THE HAUNTING OF EVIE MEYERS

RICK WOOD

BLOOD SPLATTER PRESS

ALSO BY RICK WOOD

Blood Splatter Books
Psycho B*tches
Shutter House
This Book is Full of Bodies
Home Invasion
Haunted House
Woman Scorned
This Book is Full of More Bodies
He's Always Watching Me

Cia Rose
When the World Has Ended
When the End Has Begun
When the Living Have Lost
When the Dead Have Decayed

The Edward King Series
I Have the Sight
Descendant of Hell
An Exorcist Possessed
Blood of Hope
The World Ends Tonight

Anthologies
Twelve Days of Christmas Horror
Twelve Days of Christmas Horror Volume 2
Roses Are Red So Is Your Blood

Standalones
When Liberty Dies
The Death Club

Sean Mallon
The Art of Murder
Redemption of the Hopeless

Chronicles of the Infected
Zombie Attack
Zombie Defence
Zombie World

Non-Fiction
How to Write an Awesome Novel
The Writer's Room
Horror, Demons and Philosophy

For Mum and Dad
Thank you for your support

Prologue

I need an ambulance...
     ... Now...
     ... Three people...
  ... All dead...
  ... Not breathing, I think, I—I'm not sure...
  ... My name?...
  ... I'm Moses Iscariot...
  ... Yes, I'm at...
  ... What?...
"Mo, put down the phone."
"What? I'm getting an ambulance."
"No, you are not."
"What do you mean? Of course I–"
"Just put down the damn phone."
He snatches the phone from my hand and glares at it.

I panic. Will the paramedics be able to find us? They have my name, but not the location, or the circumstance, or anything that will help to find us.

"They need an ambulance!" I demand, reaching for the phone.

Father Graham scowls at me and throws the phone out of the window. "Stop being such a child.."

"I am not a *child*."

"Of course not. You're a thirty-four-year-old idiot."

"Thirty-five."

He wipes his brow and cleans his glasses. "Then you should know better than to act irrationally."

"Irrationally? Father, these people need medical help!"

"A doctor can't help the dead. Leave them be."

Graham runs a hand through grey tufts of hair and turns back to the room. His eyes linger on one blood-sodden face, then another, like they are a puzzle to solve. He places his hands on his hips and tries to figure it out.

The wardrobe is on its side. The door smashed to pieces. Pieces of glass from the window scatter over the floor. The rope that held the girl in place is broken and frayed, the knots still around her cold, stiff wrists. Her body twists to the side. Her knees bend backwards. Her eyes are wide open, and her arms are contorted in wayward directions.

The parents lay beside their daughter. The mother is on her back with her arms splayed out and the metal railing from the bed stuck through her heart. Her husband lays next to her, blood still leaking from the open wound on his throat.

"Let's give the dead some dignity, shall we?" April says, entering the room with some blankets. She covers the girl first, then the parents, drawing a cross over their bodies as she does. She takes a moment, bows her head, then rises.

"And you're okay with this?" I ask, sure that she'll say no. If anyone is aware of the ethical implications of what we've done, it's April. She is gentle yet fierce. Full of light yet owns the dark. One of the wisest people I know. A future saint.

"It is what it is," she tells me.

"What did you just say?"

"We don't like this, Mo, but–"

"We need an ambulance."

"An ambulance cannot help them now."

I frown at her. Turn to Graham. He may be a despicable human being, but at least it doesn't make me feel sick to hear him say such things.

"So what are you going to do with the bodies?" I ask, unable to hide the accusation in my voice.

Graham shrugs. "The Church will decide."

"The Church?"

"Yes. We'll probably go with a psychotic break. Or a home invasion. It will be an easy story to sell to the public."

I turn back to April. She returns my stare, but remains silent. I expect her to say something. To say this isn't right. That people deserve to know the truth. That three people lay dead in front of us, and we can't just treat them like a problem to get rid of.

This girl was possessed. Our exorcism failed. She murdered her family.

This is *our* responsibility.

"Mo, just think about this for a moment," she says, stepping toward me. I can smell her lavender laundry detergent. Her eyes are wide, and her lips are red, and just looking at them drives me crazy.

"Think about what?"

"How would people react if we told them the truth?"

"They'd listen."

She shakes her head solemnly. "They would condemn us. We'd be imprisoned for manslaughter. People aren't ready to understand."

"Then we should make them understand."

"No, Mo. Consider how many people we've saved. If we allow ourselves to be sent to prison because of one fatality, then how will we save anyone else?"

I look at Graham, then at April. I expected this from him.

He's old and cynical, hates his calling, and spends most of his days muttering under his breath at the television. But not April.

April is strong. Wonderful. She knows what's right.

"I don't believe either of you," I say, and charge past the battered door and down the stairs. Each step moans under my heel. I cross a hallway full of shadows and step onto the porch. The welcome mat is frayed, and the w, l, c and e have faded. Hanging baskets full of dead flowers that were once beautiful hang beside the front door.

I step further away from the house, onto the driveway. Cows that no longer have an owner graze the adjacent field. I take a cigarette, light it, then hold it by my side. I don't want to smoke.

"Mo," comes April's voice behind me. She sounds like silk through fingers.

"Don't." I hold my hand up to halt her, then drop the cigarette and stub it out. I don't want her to smell the smoke on me.

"We've been doing this a lot longer than you have. In all honesty, if we had found you sooner, then you may understand better."

"That's rubbish, April. None of you even want me here; you only found me because of my lineage."

"And it's a wonderful lineage."

"Tell that to two and a half billion Christians."

She's talking about my surname. Iscariot. Evidence that I am the ancestor of Judas, the man who betrayed Jesus.

Except maybe he didn't. We know now that various gospels were omitted from the Bible, each of them telling different versions of events. This includes Judas's, which was found in 1978 by an Egyptian antiques dealer. Christianity denied its existence, and it wasn't until 2000 that someone translated it, and we learnt the truth.

At least, another version of the truth.

One where, during Passover, Jesus took Judas aside and revealed secret knowledge about God; knowledge that he only shared with Judas, believing him to be wiser than the other apostles. This was also why Jesus asked Judas to report him to the Romans instead of his other disciples. An action that would finally allow Jesus to leave his material body and become truly divine.

If this is true, then I carry the blood of an incredible man; an apostle that Christ himself deemed to be worthy of greater status, even if the world believes it belongs to a traitor.

There is often a disparity between how things are, and how popular opinion deems them to be.

"I've been fighting demons for longer than you, Mo, remember that. I was there in the war with Hell, I was there during mass possession, I was there when—"

"When your precious Oscar showed what a hero he was?"

She says nothing.

"He's the reason, isn't he?" I ask.

"I don't know what you're talking about."

"Oscar. He's why."

"Oscar has nothing to do with those deaths."

"I'm not talking about the exorcism. I'm talking about *us*."

She frowns. There is no *us*. The hardest part of unrequited love is when you know it is actually reciprocated, but they just can't see past their own damage.

"Let's go in and have a cup of tea, Mo."

"A cup of tea? Three people are dead and you're offering me a cup of tea?"

"And a person to listen. An ear to vent to. And a hand to hold."

"And what else?"

I step toward her. She recoils. I step back again. A dog howls in the distance. Or is it a wolf? I'm not sure.

"I'm leaving, April."

"Oh, don't be silly."

"I can't stay. Not after this. Not now."

"Just think it over. Take some time off, think about it, and–"

"I can't be part of a group of people who think this is okay."

A car engine grows louder in the distance. Seconds later, a Mercedes Benz speeds up the path and stops on the driveway. Three men step out—one wears a priest's collar, the other wear hazmat suits.

They look at April expectantly.

"Bedroom at the top of the stairs," she tells them, and they hustle inside.

I scoff. They arrived sooner than I thought they would.

"Unbelievable."

I turn away from April and trudge down the country path. My footsteps are loud in the silence.

"Where are you going?" April asks, but I just keep walking, and I don't look back. I don't know where I'm going, but it's not like it matters.

This is what I'm used to.

Jumping from one precarious situation to the next. From foster home to foster home. From job to job. From relationship to relationship. Nothing is ever as good as it initially appears. School was tedious and monotonous. Teachers were bored and tired, not inspirational. I got a job in construction, then plumbing, then as an electrician, then as a barista—I was good at them, but I was never *great* at them.

But when these people—these *Sensitives*—told me I have a gift, I thought maybe, just maybe, I have a purpose. This is a skill. Something I can excel at. Something that matters.

But I was wrong.

And it's time for me to leave again. From somewhere I thought I belonged—but I thought I belonged to all of them at some point, didn't I?

Sometimes I wonder what the point is.

Why keep going? Why keep living when this is all life is?

Moving from one misery to the other.

Maybe I'll give up when I can be bothered.

Or maybe I'll just wander aimlessly until the elements destroy me.

I can still hear April. She calls my name. I hear it three times.

Then she stops.

Three times, and she stops.

That's all I'm worth to her.

Three times.

Then again, I wouldn't have bothered calling my name at all.

ONE YEAR LATER

Evie Speaks

It happens at night.

I don't know how, or why, but I awake, and I run barefoot over the tufts of the carpet and onto the bumps of gravel of the street outside, led by a voice that calls through the silence.

It's soft and soundless. So faint you could mistake it for a gust of wind, or the rustle of an animal in a bin, or the rattling of a chain on a fence.

It whispers my name, over and over.

Evie... Evie...

It entices me closer, and I follow it. I don't know why. It's just too beautiful. I can almost see the outline of a finger waving me toward the absence. It's a kind, smooth hand. Ringless and unbroken.

It's a mother's hand.

I look back at my bedroom window. The faint glow of my nightlight changes the shade of my curtains to orange. The flat itself is two floors up, nestled between dozens of other council flats. Some windows are boarded up. There are a few broken pots with wilted, dead plants. It's so far away that, if I reach my arm out, I can pretend to grab our flat in my fist.

I keep moving, and it isn't long until all those flats disappear through distance and darkness.

I'm not sure how I make it so far. I don't even realise I'm walking.

I've brought the crucifix Mummy gave me on my sixteenth birthday, just a few weeks ago, which I grip tightly in my palm, only this time, instead of spreading Christ's love through my body, it burns my hand. Still, I don't let go. I refuse to think that He is denying me His love, so I grip harder, wincing at the pain, and it isn't until a grey smoke rises from my palm and above clouds of my breath that I drop the crucifix, and stare at the red imprint left in my hand from what usually gives me strength.

Evie... Evie...

It comes from the trees. They branches sway like a dancer that can't keep in time. My feet are wet from the puddles. I pass a few beer cans and a cigarette butt and a discarded Durex box, then I reach grass, which is soft and kind to my feet.

I glance over my shoulder. The full moon hides behind the trees. There are no streetlamps. No car lights. No torches. I am alone in the darkness.

Though I am not alone, am I?

I can still hear her calling for me.

Evie... Evie...

I keep moving farther away from the block of flats, away from the nostalgia of a hundred childhood memories, and toward the dark green leaves and branches that arrange themselves like broken limbs.

Evie... Come...

I am so far among the trees that I cannot see a thing. I feel dirty and soil clings to my toes. If I stretch my hand out, I can use the coarse indents of tree trunks to guide me. I can smell damp moss and animal dung, but all I can see are various shades of black.

Evie... You're almost there...

"Who are you?"

I'm surprised by the childish wonder in my voice. I don't convey any fear. Then again, I don't feel any. What I am doing is right, not foolish. I am edging closer toward the warmest love that has ever existed, and as soon as I reach the voice, it will envelope me in its arms and make me feel safe and wanted and like I never need to look for love in anyone else again.

Evie... You're so close...

The rustle of leaves and the snap of a twig mark my route. I am in the middle of a labyrinth of nature, getting ever closer to the one who will protect me.

Mummy protects me, though.

I know she does.

For sixteen years, she has protected me.

You're lying...

What?

No, I'm not.

I can't be.

Mummy has protected me.

She has always protected me.

She walks me to school. She meets me at the end of the day. She comes to parent's evenings. She always gives me a reward when we arrive home.

Always.

You're lying...

Well, there was that one parent's evening...

The teacher asked if I could step away for a moment. I opened my book but didn't read it; I watched them from afar instead. I could see them talking about me. I heard words such as "concerned" and "no friends" and "not included" and "doesn't fit in."

No boy has ever broken my heart, but that's because Mummy won't let them.

No friend has ever invited me to their home, but that's because Mummy says they are all jealous.

She cuts gum out of my hair and puts plasters on my cuts and says nothing to the school, but that's because Mummy wants me to *fit in more,* and she thinks telling teachers would make things worse.

She protects me in her own way.

Stop walking.

I stop walking. I wipe my eyes. There are tears on my sleeve. I can't see them, but I feel their weight.

Spread your arms.

I lift my arms out. The sleeves of my pyjama top dangle. I can't see the teddy bears that decorate my nightwear, but I know they are there, just as I know that *she's* there, and I know *she* loves me.

Lift your chin.

I lift my chin. Something strokes my neck. Tracks its circumference with an affectionate stroke.

Widen your legs.

I spread my legs until I am standing like a star.

The wind brushes against me from behind. Its breath flicks my hair forward. I don't move, because I know I'm not supposed to.

This is when it happens. I don't feel the ground anymore. I am inches above it, with my feet hanging limply.

Close your eyes.

I close my eyes.

She runs her hand down my chest, between my breasts, and across my navel. I feel the cold against my buttocks, and then I feel something slithering, like a worm, up my calves, and I tense, and suddenly I don't feel like *she's* quite so loving anymore.

"I don't want to–"

My voice is muffled. There's a hand over my mouth. I try to move, but I can't. I am stuck, hovering above the earth, and I feel it move up my thighs, not so much like a snake but like a long worm, finding its way inside of me. It's small, at first, then it gets bigger. It thickens. And I feel it moving up, flexing around my ovaries, spreading through my colon, wrapping around my lungs and my heart, through my throat until I choke.

My body tenses. It's uncomfortable, even painful, at first. Then I get used to it.

Then I fall, and I land on my knees, but the leaves cushion my fall.

I roll onto my side, and this is where I rest, wrapping my arms around my legs, shivering, shaking.

When I wake up, I'm not sure what happened.

Whether I sleepwalked.

Whether I was dreaming.

Whether I imagined it all. I just know that I'm outside.

A dog sniffs my face and licks my nose. I open my eyes and a man is asking if I'm okay. The sun has risen and I can see again.

I sit up. Look around. There are patches of mud over my pyjamas, and my hands and feet are covered in dirt.

"Yes, I…"

I don't quite know what to tell him.

After he's helped me home, a hand resting on my back as I walk, huddled over, trying to make sense of which part of my memory is true. My mother wraps a towel around me and thanks the man profusely.

I have a bath and I get ready for school and, once I am clean, with warm clothes on, I feel better.

Still, my body seems to weigh more. I feel like I'm carrying around something heavy, but I'm still as thin as I was. My legs feel like they are wading through water and my arms feel like they are carrying heavy shopping bags.

Mummy asks if I should stay at home today. I say no, as I

have music class, and that's my favourite. She says okay, but I can call her any time if I want her to pick me up.

I walk into registration and sit by myself, as I do most lessons and at lunch, and the clarity of the previous night lessens even more. It's like a dream I remembered when I woke up, but keeps fading every time I think about it. Now, I only have glimpses, none of which makes enough sense that I can articulate them.

Despite it being the first time I've ever sleepwalked, it occurs again every two or three weeks, and I awake in the same place every time.

And every time, I remember less and less, but feel heavier and heavier.

But *she* never stops whispering to me, and I never think to ignore *her*.

She says she will not be ignored.

She says she loves me.

She says that she'll be my friend, even if no one else will.

And, to be honest, I kind of like it.

ONE

The sound of a client flushing the chemical toilet is all that can be heard in my boss's office.

I say 'office'—it's a cabin. The radiator takes up most of it, and occasionally makes a random cranking noise. There are posters on the wall advertising psychic events that happened over a year ago, the windows are too stiff to open, and the floor feels uneven.

Jules is on the phone, sat at his desk—or, at least, what he calls his desk. It's an old table he shoved in the corner and put a phone and computer on. He gesticulates his fat hand at me in a way that I think means *sit down and wait*, so I find the plastic chair with the least stains and sit down.

It's not a great feeling, knowing I'm about to be fired from a job I hate.

I didn't know what other job I was supposed to do. I have a gift that allows me to manipulate the paranormal, control demons, and see things that other people can't see. When I saw a job advertised for a psychic, predicting people's futures, I looked past the tacky crystal ball they assigned me and figured I would at least be using some of my ability. After a two-day training course on cold-reading, I began to wonder whether I was going to use my gift at all.

But I did. I gave people guidance that would help them, then went to get a cup of coffee and listened to my colleagues laughing about what nonsense they told their clients. One colleague told a young woman, "You are often outgoing when with friends, but find yourself more introverted when alone", and laughed at how she thought this was a profound insight, and not just a loose statement that would apply to most of us.

I've avoided this. I have always looked at a client and tried to sense the energy around them; to sense what kind of spirits cling onto them. Most had good spirits, or deceased family members watching over them. It's always reassured them to hear this.

Then came today's session.

As soon as the woman entered, I felt it. Something dark. I could smell the decay. The aroma of rotting eggs that often precedes an onslaught of evil. She sat in front of me with her long, blond hair down to her elbows, her tie-dyed skirt flowing over the sides of the seat, and a pendant hanging from a piece of string around her neck.

I know her type.

Hippyish. Consider themselves spiritual. Says things they think are profound but are just ridiculous. Like, "people who want to kill themselves are just angels who want to go home," or, "war doesn't decide who is right, only who is left." Such statements sound deep, but the more I think about them, the more they sound like nonsense.

"Take a seat," I told her.

"This one?" she asks, despite it being the only seat that I'm not sitting in.

"Yes."

I took her hands and placed my thumb and forefinger on either side of her palm. I closed my eyes. It struck me straight away; the image of something ominous, something sinister. When I opened my eyes again, I saw it. Small, the head of an owl and body of an angel, straddling a wolf, holding a sword.

Its name was Andras. I'd met this demon before, only last time I'd met it, it was in a seven-year-old boy, not a forty-something woman.

And Andras hadn't only just chosen her, either. The demon had been following her for a while. It was absorbing her, entering her body, and becoming her. Demonic possession would follow shortly and, if the possession lasted long enough, amalgamation incarnation would follow—the process by which a demon robs a human of its place on earth; it is what happens when a demon isn't dealt with soon enough, and is often misinterpreted as insanity. She needed an immediate exorcism.

But I don't do exorcisms.

Not anymore.

I had no obligation to tell her. No duty. It was my job to make people feel positive.

But I couldn't let her go without warning her.

"There is something attached to you."

She looked a little confused.

"Something... good?"

"Listen closely, there isn't much time. Its name is Andras, it's a demon, and if you don't deal with it soon, then you will no longer—"

Andras screeched, and I quickly covered my ears. She looked confused. That's when I realised she hadn't heard it.

"What's going on?" she asked. "Is this a joke?"

"Listen, if you don't deal with this soon, you're going to die."

She left the room a few minutes later in floods of tears. I watched as she went into my boss's cabin.

I know this woman will do nothing about this demon and will end up hurting someone, probably within months.

And now here I am. Gazing at the cracked walls and smudged windows of a room where no one aspires to end up.

Jules puts the phone down. Turns to me. Shakes his head. Raises his eyebrows like I'm a child and he's a head teacher, and not a loser with an ego.

"What the fuck, Moses?" he asks, the excess skin on his neck wobbling as he talks.

I consider telling him the truth. Then I just shrug instead.

"Did you really tell that woman that she was going to *die*?"

"I, er... yeah. I did, I guess."

"What are you, some kind of sick fuck?"

"No, Jules, I'm not a sick fuck." I look down and fiddle with my jacket's zipper. I hate how someone so pathetic can make me feel so small. I stop fiddling and look up, telling myself not to let him intimidate me.

"But what the hell do you think we're doing here?"

"Predicting futures. Telling people's auras. Helping people?"

"Yes, exactly, *helping* people. Not scaring the shit out of them. I mean, what the fuck, man? Are you trying to put me out of business or what? We have a duty to leave these people happy about their shitty lives and the shitty direction they are going."

"And what about our duty to the truth?"

He frowns at me. "What truth? There is no fucking truth."

"Not the way you do it."

He snorts a sarcastic laugh. I notice some icing from a donut on the collar of his shirt. "You really think you have some ability the rest of us do not, don't you?"

I go to answer, then don't. What would be the point? Would he believe me if I said yes?

"Get the fuck out of here," he tells me.

I stand. Traipse to the door. Turn back.

"Am I–"

"Fired? Of course you fucking are. You told a woman she was going to fucking die. Now get the fuck out of my office."

I open the door. Consider making a comment about his office, like how he should think again before calling it that— but I can see his reply: *And what office do you have?*

And he'd be right.

I have a long walk home to my council flat where I will find a small television, stale food, and rowdy neighbours on the other side of a wall that seems as thin as cardboard.

And now I don't even have a job.

I leave, shutting the door behind me, and wrap my coat around myself. They say it's due to be minus six degrees tonight. It feels like that already.

Two

I approach the block of council flats I call home, traipsing through the car park with my head down to avoid being noticed. Clothes hang from railings, still wet in the cold air. Window frames that used to be white are now cracked and grey. Satellite dishes are outside most flats, despite most of the residents being unable to buy Christmas presents for their children.

I drag my feet up the exterior set of stairs until I reach the second floor. The council has installed more CCTV. Someone's graffitied *fuck da police* on a freshly painted wall. No matter how many residents complain about the state of the estate, as soon as the council does anything about it, someone goes and ruins it all over again.

I reach the exterior of the flats on the second floor. I pass window after window, trying not to look inside, though it's hard not to notice what's going on at the edge of my peripheral vision. One man is shouting at his wife, and his voice is as audible as if he was standing next to me. Another is watching daytime television whilst their kid wanders around in a nappy.

An old man gets dressed with no thought for his dignity, his skin hanging off his bones as he forces his spindly legs into beige trousers.

I turn the corner and approach my door. I stare ahead and keep walking.

And I pause as I pass my next-door neighbour.

I'm not sure what it is, but something makes me stop.

I turn my head slightly. Listen. The house is silent. Eerily so, when compared to the raucous noise coming from most other flats. There is a mat outside the door with the silhouette of a poodle on it. A few plant pots line the wall beneath the living room window, but I can't tell what flowers used to be in them; every stem and petal has wilted and died.

But it's not what I hear, or what I see.

It's what I feel.

A churning in my gut. My stomach flutters, giving me a feeling of nerves, like I'm about to go on stage and I don't know my lines.

Whatever's inside this home is not good. It's infesting the family who live here. And the family doesn't know.

I consider knocking.

But what would I say?

Hi, just wanted to let you know I think your family is consumed by evil. See you later...

Nothing good would come out of telling them. Either they won't believe me, and the community will think I'm crazy and dangerous—or they believe me, and I have to help them fight it.

I'm not that guy anymore.

I pass the flat and place the key in my front door. The lock grinds as I twist it. The door is stiff and I have to use my shoulder to push it open. Once inside, I lock the door and put the latch on.

There is no mail by my feet. No other pairs of shoes on the shoe rack. No delightful aroma of a well-cooked meal coming from the kitchen. Just silence and darkness.

I take off my jacket and throw it on the sofa as I pass through the living room. I knock over a few DVDs I have stacked on the floor. The room doesn't have space for a book-case, so I store them in the corners. I'm not sure why I bother, I never watch them.

I enter the kitchen. The floor is uneven. The plaster has cracked. I open the fridge. Inside is a half-cut lemon with mould around its edge, a microwave meal that expired yester-day, and a half-empty box of beer. I take a beer, open the can, and take a large gulp as I close the fridge door with my back.

I don't even taste it anymore.

I used to love beer. I even went to a real ale festival, back when I had someone to go with. Now the taste doesn't matter, just whether the percentage of alcohol is high enough.

I leave the kitchen and find my way to the sofa. A broken spring prods me through the cushion. I move over to avoid it.

I look for my remote control. It's not on the armrest, or under the cushion, or under the sofa.

It's on the windowsill.

Next to the only picture I have.

I try to ignore the picture, but I can't, and as I get up to retrieve the remote, I'm unable to avoid the cheerful smiles of my parents. It is a lie captured in a perfect moment and immortalised forever. I don't know why I keep it there.

I put the television on. Some degenerates are shouting at each other in front of an audience. The caption at the bottom reads *The Mistress Who Ruined My Marriage*. I turn the volume down, and my gaze wanders back to the photograph.

My mother has her arms around my father as he sits at a table. Their smiles show teeth. Their skin is unblemished. It's odd, as I don't remember my dad ever having clear skin. It could be true about my mother, though. I never knew her at all. She died giving birth to me.

Dad talked about her a lot. Well, maybe not a lot, but from time to time. He'd open up about her, about her generosity, about her good spirit, about her enthusiasm for helping people—then he'd look at me. The constant reminder of why she was dead. And he'd fall silent. And I wouldn't ask questions.

I never knew a time when my father wasn't an alcoholic, but my mother did. I often wonder how different the man she knew was from the man I knew. Whether he was dignified instead of abusive. Easy-going instead of high maintenance. Kind instead of angry.

Most days, I barely saw him. He worked nights, so I was left to walk myself to school. Parents would look at me and wonder who would let a child so young walk to school on their own. Sometimes a friend's parent—from what few friends I had—would walk closely behind to make sure I arrived at school safely. No one ever questioned Dad.

Then again, they never saw the bruises.

He wasn't that abusive. He rarely hurt me. It was usually on the anniversary of my mother's death. Most kids would get a party on their birthday—I'd get a reminder that I was the reason for the state of his life. I remember even buying my own cake once. I hid it from Dad because he never wanted to celebrate.

I know I could have seen him as a nasty, spiteful man—but I didn't. I saw him as a man in pain.

So instead of hating him, I would wait until he passed out on the sofa, and I'd tidy away the empty beer bottles, and I'd take his slippers off, and I'd put a blanket over him, and place a bucket by his head in case he was sick.

In the last few years of his life, he never hit me. He never hugged me either. Sometimes I wished he would do either, but he didn't. He neither loved me nor hated me. He felt something far worse—indifference. Blissfully content to feeling nothing. I was just someone who lived in his home.

Just like April. She doesn't love me or hate me. She feels nothing, and that's what kills me. Sometimes I think I'd rather someone screamed in my face than walk away and shrug their shoulders.

Perhaps I never realised how much I needed my father until the day he killed himself. I waited three hours after I arrived home before getting help. I was eight—I didn't know what to do.

I stand up. Turn the photo frame face down. I don't want them to look at me anymore. I pause at the window until a lad in a grubby vest walks by and scowls at me. He has a shaved head and tribal tattoos from his wrist to the top of his neck. I return to the sofa.

I pick up my phone. I know the number I want to call, but I also know how pathetic it makes me feel.

Well, how pathetic it makes me feel *afterwards*. When I realise that she's only with me for one reason. Like Dad. Like April.

But for the hour that precedes the misery, she is mine, and she loves me with a fiery passion, and if I really try, I can actually believe that.

The phone rings for a while before she picks up. I ask her if she's coming round. She says she's busy tonight. I say I'll pay her a little more. She says fine, she'll be around, but a little later than usual. I say that's fine, I'm not going anywhere.

And I sit and wait, watching television as the darkness outside grows more intense. Shouts come from the car park; blokes being rowdy with each other, making comments about passing women, drinking from beer cans that will decorate the ground in the morning.

I get up once to shut the curtains.

It's almost midnight by the time she gets here.

Evie Speaks

I don't know what's happening.

I'm sat in science class. Everyone else is working in pairs and I'm working alone. The teachers don't even question it. Any time they ask the class to get into groups, they accept that I am the unspoken exception to this request. That I will remain sat on my stool, my pencil case full of stationery, ready to work hard but to do it in alone.

I collect my safety mat. My tripod. My metal tongs. My safety goggles. My bunsen burner. Our teacher told us last lesson that they were named after Robert Bunsen, who was born in 1811, a man who was elected as a member of the Swedish Academy of Sciences, even though he wasn't Swedish.

I take my equipment back to my desk. By the time I arrive, the teacher has placed a small piece of paper with instructions for the experiment on the table, just as she has everyone else.

As I survey the instructions, I hear sniggering. I glance up and Stacey turns her back to me. She's been given permission to work in a three. This is so no one has to work with me. Her long, blond ponytail flies through the air as she turns her head from one friend to the other. I don't know her friend's names.

Stacey says something and they turn to look at me and laugh. "What a loser," they say. Then they turn back to their experiment, still laughing. It's high-pitched and girlish and irritating.

Mummy says that girls do this because they are jealous. That I should rise above it.

The teachers say I should tell them when things like this happen, even though it changes nothing.

She says I shouldn't let people push me around like this. I tell her that there's nothing I can do, and I return to the instructions.

1/ Draw a table in your book with two headings and six rows to write your results. Label the left column *Ion Present* and label the right column *Flame Colour*.

I take out my ruler and pencil. You should always draw tables in pencil, not pen. I give two lines for each row. Then I label the columns in blue pen, careful to put capital letters in the same places as written in the instructions.

She whispers in my ear as I do this. *She* tells me we're worth more than Stacey. *She* says we should show Stacey how worthless she really is.

I tell *her* that Mummy says to rise above it. That violence solves nothing.

She tells me that Mummy is lying.

And I tell *her* she's wrong.

2/ Collect your first metal ion from the front of the class. You can choose between lithium, sodium, potassium, calcium, barium and copper.

I walk to the front of class. Most people have started with the first, lithium, so I start with the last, copper.

When I arrive back, there's something on my book. At the

bottom of the page. In scruffy handwriting, *your a FKin lOOOOser.* I know it wasn't me, as I would spell it 'you're.'

I look up. Stacey glances over her shoulder. She giggles with her friends again.

I rip the page from my book and redraw the table. I use pencil and ruler again, and make sure it is just as neat.

3/ Hold the metal ion over the flame using the tongs and note down the colour of the flame. Make sure you are wearing safety goggles.

I put the safety goggles on. They are big and plastic and tight and dirty. I can barely see out of them. And they get attached to my hair. I try taking them off, and the goggles lift a few strands of my hair. I pull and I finally take the safety goggles away to find chewing gum on the inside of the strap.

Stacey is laughing again. She and her friends are in hysterics.

She tells me I know what I should do.

She tells me *she* knows what I should do.

But *she* doesn't. I just want to do the experiment. I want to see what colour the flame changes with ion copper.

I find a new pair of safety goggles. There's only one pair left, and it has a large smudge over the front and the straps are even tighter. I put it on and return to my desk. I lift the ion copper between the tongs. I hold it over the flame and watch in awe as the flame changes to a bluish green. It's beautiful. Like if the depths of the ocean were fire instead of water. In the blurs above the flame, Stacey's head loses focus. I watch it intently, unable to remove my gaze.

"Evie?"

The copper burns harder and I put it deeper into the flame, watching the colour grow more intense.

"Evie?"

The flame is stunning.

The flame is magic.

The flame is how we should do it.

"Evie!"

I quickly lift my head up. My teacher is standing over me. She tells me that once I've observed the colour, I need to note it down. To stop wasting time.

"Yes, Miss," I say, and I place the tongs and the ion copper on the safety mat and return to the table I drew earlier. I write in to the first row of the left column, *Copper, CU^2*, and in the right column, *bluish green.*

Then I return to my instructions.

4/ After you have finished noting down the first colour, use the Bunsen Burner to set fire to Stacey's hair.

I thought I'd be getting the next bit of ion first, but okay.

I walk around the other side of the table so I am directly behind Stacey. I pick up the Bunsen Burner, and the tubing is the perfect length from the gas tap to be able to hold it beneath Stacey's ponytail.

Slowly, I lift it, until the edge of the flame meets the tip of her perfect, long hair. It singes a little. There is a little smoke.

I lift the Bunsen Burner higher until the entire flame is in Stacey's hair. It takes longer than I'd thought it would to produce flames, but it does eventually.

When Stacey's friend turns around, sees me and screams, that's when I realise what I'm doing, and I quickly put the Bunsen Burner back on the safety mat and look around, as if there's an answer hidden in the room as to why I just did that.

When Stacey notices, she screams too, and she rushes around the classroom, scampering back and forth, like an insane chicken, until eventually the teacher gets hold of her arms, takes her to the tap, and pours water over the hair.

The flames die out, but there is a large chunk of hair missing on the end of the ponytail, and it has turned to black. Smoke attacks the air. There is a smell of rotting, but I'm not sure if I'm imagining it.

She thinks I did well.

I'm not sure what to think.

"Who did this?" the teacher demands. "Well?"

"She did, Miss! It was her!"

The girl who'd been sitting next to Stacey jabs her finger in my direction. It's inches from my face and *she* says I should bite it off.

The teacher frowns. She's perplexed. She doesn't quite believe it.

"Are you sure?" she asks.

"Yes, Miss, it was her, I saw it!"

"Are you sure it wasn't an accident?"

"It was her, Miss!"

"But it's not like Evie."

The teacher turns to me. I still can't remember her name. Her head tilts to the side and I can feel all the eyes of the rest of the class burning into me with their gaze, all desperate to find out if it's true—whether or not I am a psycho.

"Did you do this, Evie?" the teacher asks. "Did you set Stacey's hair on fire?"

I don't know what to say.

She tells me it's fine. That *she'll* protect me. That there's nothing they can do.

But I'm not quite sure I remember doing it, even though I think I did.

"I don't know," I say, though the words are silent and barely pass my lips.

"Say that again, Evie."

"I... don't know." I'm a little louder this time, but it's little more than a whisper.

"What do you mean, you don't know?" Stacey's friend shouts. "I saw you! How do you not know if you set her hair on fire!"

"That's enough."

"But Miss–"

"I said that's enough."

Miss turns to Stacey, who remains by the sink, glaring at me with only a little more detestation than the rest of the class. She wipes her eyes and *we* don't buy it for a moment.

"Perhaps you ought to sit this lesson out, Evie," the teacher tells me.

I want to object. To say I was looking forward to this experiment. That I want to learn, I want to know what colour the other ions turn the flame.

We want to tell her that Stacey deserves it.

As it is, I pick up my book, pencil case and bag, and I shuffle out, feeling the scowls and hearing the whispers. They are nothing new. Everyone whispers when my back is turned. It's not like I'm going to lose any friends over this.

Miss guides me into an office and gives me a worksheet to do. I finish it in ten minutes, even though it says it should take twenty. I don't return to the classroom to ask for another one, though I know I should. I don't want everyone looking at me again.

I can tell she doesn't know what to make of it. Who to believe. She knows no one likes me, but I've never done anything bad before. Mummy says I don't have a bad bone in my body.

She says that I did well.

And *we* stay here, hidden away, as the bell goes and my classmates shuffle out, some of them trying to look through the window to marvel at me like I'm a tiger in a zoo.

Stacey never bothers me again.

THREE

I lay naked on top of the duvet, my belly a small bump sticking out from my otherwise flat body. I should change these bedsheets, but that would mean going to the laundrette. Besides, it's not like anyone else is going to be around to smell them, and after a while, I just get used to it.

Ramona sits on the edge of the bed, pulling up her bra straps and tightening the clasp behind her back. Her underwear is black and lacy. She takes her tights and rolls them up her first leg. Those legs are perfect.

All of her is perfect.

She pauses. Turns back at me. She can feel me watching. I don't care; I enjoy looking at her.

"How come you don't have any photos on the wall or nothing?" she asks. I'm annoyed by the question. It's her job to make me feel good, not to make me feel ashamed.

"I don't have any to put up."

"No family or anything?"

I don't answer.

"I mean, it could maybe use a fresh coat of paint or something."

"You fancy doing it?"

"That's not what you pay me for."

"Then quit commenting on the state of my flat."

I know I'm curt, but I don't want a lecture. Besides, she's not wrong. The walls are pale and there are more cracks than I can count. The wardrobe came secondhand from a charity shop and has never lost its smell of damp; I can smell it on every piece of clothing I wear.

"What about some posters?" she asks. "What's your favourite movie?"

I shrug. "Don't really watch movies."

"Favourite band?"

"I don't have one."

"Favourite book then?"

"Why would I want posters up? I'm not a teenager."

"I have posters on my wall."

"How old are you?"

"Nineteen."

"Exactly."

She chuckles. I love the sound of her laugh, even when it's mocking me. She finds her dress. Lifts it over her head and slides it down her body. I hate watching her body go. It's like a set of perfect shapes entwined. Her skin is mixed-race, a gentle shade of light brown.

Still, her dress is red. She always looks good in red.

"Are you married?" she asks, searching for her purse. She finds it under the bed.

"Do I look married?"

"Have you ever been married?"

I don't answer.

She looks at me, waiting.

I still don't answer.

"Fine," she says. She sounds playful, though I'm sure she's

annoyed. "I'm just going to use your bathroom, then I'm gone."

She leaves the room and I hear the lock of the bathroom door.

She doesn't need to know I was married once. She doesn't need to know it was foolish. She doesn't need to know any of it.

I take my mobile phone from the floor beside the bed. It's an old iPhone model on which most apps don't work anymore. I open Facebook and click on the search bar. My ex-wife's name is the first that comes up. I click on it.

Her profile picture is new. Her kids are in it. Two boys and a girl. She has her arms around them. She's in a garden. The grass is short, and the shed is new. In her cover photo, she is with a husband I've never met. He's not even the guy who broke up our marriage. What a waste of love that was.

I was nineteen when we got married. It was too young, but I was desperate for a place where I belonged, and I guess I saw her as that place. I tried my best, but it wasn't good enough. Besides, I'm a tough person to live with, even more so back then. She left me after two years for a guy she met in a nightclub. He was twenty years older than her, had been divorced twice, and had four kids and no job. It didn't hurt that she left me, I expected that—everyone leaves in the end—it was just who she left me for. Am I such a loser that she'd dump me for such a poor prospect?

Then again, maybe she was right. Maybe he was better than me. Maybe anyone was, and she just needed an excuse.

They broke up a year later, and she met the guy who's now her husband. I think they met through internet dating. She wore a white dress with a long trail on her wedding day and her father walked her down the aisle. I'd never seen her father smile, but he was smiling in a clip someone had uploaded to

Facebook. Her husband has a defined chin and works in finance.

There isn't a single photo of them together where they aren't both smiling.

The toilet flushes, and I put the phone away. I take some cash out of the bedside drawer and count it. When Ramona returns, I hand her the cash, and she checks the amount but doesn't thank me.

"I've got to go," she says. "But this has been fun."

"You don't have to say that."

"I'm not just saying that."

"It's two minutes past the hour. Our time is up. The performance is over. It's fine."

She leans over me and drops her lips to mine. She kisses me gently, with such soft affection that I can only just feel them. But I know they are there.

"Consider that a freebie," she whispers, and I hate her for ruining the illusion. That kiss felt like love. Now it just feels like a game.

She stands and walks to the bedroom door, her arse swaying from side to side. I'm not sure if it's deliberate. She says she can see herself out, but I never intended to get up in the first place.

I hear the click of her heels in the narrow hallway, then the front door opens and closes.

Then there's silence.

Screaming, screeching, roaring silence.

And I lay in my filth, too lethargic to have a piss. My semen has left a dark patch on the grey duvet, and the used condom is on the floor.

I look at my alarm clock. It's 1.05 a.m. I don't know why I care. I hardly need to be up in the morning.

I close my eyes and, eventually, the alcohol in my system does its job, and I am dead to the world.

Four

The morning arrives, and I have nowhere to go. Yesterday, I had a job—now I have nothing. So I stay in bed. Watch the ceiling. Listen to the noise as unemployed yobs gather on the benches outside the flats, talking loudly and with multiple obscenities.

Not that I should mock the unemployed, seeing as I'm now one of them.

I turn my head. 9:57 a.m. I could get up. Then again, I could not. I could stay in bed until sores grow on my back. Close my eyes until it gets too late to have lunch and I have to go straight to dinner. What would I even be getting up for?

I had a purpose, once.

And I lost that purpose because of my morals.

Typical actions of a fool; using morals to destroy their life. Too many people have destroyed themselves over what is right, and what is wrong.

After another half an hour lying with my eyes closed, I decide I'll work on the car today. Not that there's much to be done with it. I just like spending time around it. When Dad died, he left so much debt that I didn't see a penny from the house—it all went to the various banks and credit cards he owed money to. The only thing left for me was his 1965 Ford Mustang.

The car is a wreck. Turning its ignition prompts a loud crank, there are 180,000 miles on the clock, and I can't think of a single garage that would pass its MOT without an enormous bill.

Despite this, I could probably get a six-figure sum for a car like that.

But I'll never sell it.

I will just work on it. Twist a few bolts, polish the body, sit on the driver's seat.

It's the only way I can be close to him.

Dad used to love this car. He'd take me for rides in it, going nowhere in particular. I'd sit in the passenger seat, staring at him, and in one of the few instances I can remember thinking it, I'd tell myself *he's my hero*. I'd ignore his bruised knuckles and the swelling on my leg, and I'd meet his smile with mine, and suddenly my life wouldn't be so bad.

I sit up, rotate out of bed, and place my bare feet on the ground, tufts of carpet sticking between my toes. I consider taking a shower but decide to save on the water bill. I put on an old pair of jeans—as if any of my pairs of jeans don't count as *old*—and a white t-shirt with a few oil stains that I don't mind getting wrecked. I grab a chocolate bar from the fridge, make a coffee and put it in a flask, then leave the flat.

The outside corridor smells of cannabis. The clouds above are overcast and grey. I lock my door and pause beside the rusty bannister.

There they are. Five or six blokes, already surrounded by empty cans of Stella Artois. It's not even midday and they are already pissed and aggressive. They look like a group of apes showing off, sticking their chests out and strutting, each one competing to be the alpha male, each one doing everything they can to intimidate passers-by and prove that their masculinity is the most toxic.

I pass next door. Slow down a little. I can still feel it. Something brewing. But it's not my business, so I walk on, though I am sure I catch someone's eyes through the window. A lady who looks older than she probably is. Then again, that describes most people on this estate.

I walk down the steps and into the car park. The cars are either old bangers people can't afford to replace, or shiny new sports cars that people on this estate shouldn't be able to afford. I wonder how many are stolen, then remind myself not to be so judgemental.

Dad's Mustang is in a parking space away from other cars, as if the other vehicles are trying to keep their distance. Its shape is so unlike modern cars—modern cars are constrained by laws and regulations that mean they just don't design cars like this anymore. Its body is red with two thick white stripes running over the hood and the roof, it has a small figure of a horse between the headlights, and the silver of the wheels still shines from the work I did on it at the weekend.

I open the door and sit inside, the leather seats sinking beneath the empty weight of my body. The seats are light brown, with lines of red running up the sides—a colour scheme reflected by the light brown below the red dashboard.

Between the two front seats is a compartment that I lift, revealing a set of cassette tapes—all of them Dad's. There are all the classics we used to listen to. Sinatra, Elvis, Sex Pistols. I remember hot summer days, cruising along country lanes with the windows down, Johnny Rotten mocking the queen and England's future with his trademark don't-give-a-shit voice belting out of the speakers at top volume.

There are a few obscure artists that I wouldn't know about if it weren't for Dad, too—Mike Dee & The Jaywalkers, Sonny Stewart & the Dynamos, Pat Cresswell & The Cresters. I used to make believe that I was in a band. We were called Moses Iscariot & the Reign of Fire. I stopped imagining it when I asked Dad if I could get guitar lessons and he told me it would be pointless, as I'd just be shit anyway.

I take his Jerry Lee Lewis tape and put it in. I make sure the volume is low so as not to disturb anyone in their flat. Great Balls of Fire provides me with a little background ambience as I step out of the car and contemplate what to work on today.

I walk around the front of the car until I reach the passenger side, then I halt.

My body tenses.

Sick lurches to my throat.

What the hell is that?

I look away and look back again, not sure I've seen this correctly.

But I have.

I cover my face. If I pretend it's not there, then maybe it won't be. Maybe I'm wrong.

But when I open my eyes, I'm not wrong. It's still there. Six clear letters marked on the side of the vehicle.

FAGGOT.

Each letter is green and takes up the entire height of the door.

Who would do this?

I know I'm not liked by the lads who hang around the estate. I'm usually alone, and I keep myself to myself—which is a sure way to be labelled as a weirdo. But do they hate me enough to do this?

I think of Dad's face. How red it would be. How he'd charge home and take whatever weapon he could find—

whether it be a cricket bat, a hammer, a knife—and he would march out, and would not return home until he'd found the culprits and battered them until they apologised.

I want to do the same. I want to find the lads who stare at me and whisper behind my back, and scoff when they walk past my window. I want to demand that they tell me if they did this, then beat them until they weep and beg me to stop.

I want to destroy them until they show themselves for the weak little fools they are.

But then what?

I bow my head. I hate being the one who rises above it, but that's all I can do.

I go back to my flat. Get a bucket and fill it with soapy water. Collect a sponge, walk back to the car, and start scrubbing.

The paint is tough to remove, and I have to scrub hard. I imagine they did the graffiti at least a day ago. Which also means that many people have walked past and seen what they have done to the car, which makes me angrier. I try to quell it. No good can come out of being angry. Dad taught me that.

I'm only halfway through the A when I hear chuckling from behind me. Footsteps approach, and I glance over my shoulder, and there they are. Five men. I say men—they are just overgrown boys. Resting their hands inside their tracksuit bottoms. White vests and tribal tattoos. Shaved lines across the side of their hair. Walking with a swagger like they think they are in a rap video.

They look at each other. Pretend to cover their mouths as they laugh. Two of them do a slick, sideways high five.

I want to say, *I know it was you, and I will break your neck next time*. But, truth is, I won't. What can I do against that many?

So I stay quiet. And I take it. And I watch them disappear

across the car park, still sniggering, still looking back at me until they are out of sight.

And I apologise to Dad.

I know what he'd want me to do, but I am not him.

Please, don't let me ever be him.

Five

By the time evening arrives, I am hungry and dripping with sweat. I have some pulled pork in the fridge and a bap I think hasn't gone stale yet. I stand, wiping perspiration onto my sleeve, and survey the damage.

I've gotten rid of the graffiti, but have also rubbed some of the paint off, though it's not easily noticeable. I still hate that there is damage to this car. Maybe I ought to pay for a garage to store it in. Then again, what money can I do that with?

I hate the pricks who did this. So much. What's the worse that could happen if I grab a bat and go after them? Maybe it would teach them not to mess with me.

Or maybe they'd grow in numbers and come back to find me.

Or maybe I'd end up in prison.

Or maybe I'd end up like Dad.

There's a bottle of IPA next to the pulled pork. I'm as thirsty as I am hungry. There's nothing else I can do for the Mustang. I need to stop ruminating. Maybe I'll call Romana. Or maybe I'll just watch some porn—it's cheaper.

Then again, I need internet for that. I'm pretty sure they cut my internet off last week.

I pour the remains of the bucket down a drain and return up the stairs, pulling my heavy legs to the second floor. When I reach it, I look over the banister, and I see them. Crushing their beer cans and dropping them on the ground. Destroying their community.

I turn away, both to avoid making eye contact and to avoid getting angry. I walk around the corner with my head down and bump into someone just before I reach my door.

"I'm so sorry," I say.

"Oh, it's okay," the woman says. I recognise her. She's the woman I saw earlier, through the window next door.

"You live next to me, don't you?" she asks.

I nod. Glance at my door. I don't want small talk.

"I can't believe it's been this long and we've never met," she persists. "I'm Grace. Grace Meyers."

She offers me a hand. I reluctantly take it. Her handshake is limp. Her hair is matted and greying prematurely. There are bags under her eyes. She carries a piece of paper in a hand that shakes slightly.

"And what's your name?"

"Mo."

"Mo? Short for Moses?"

"Yeah."

"And what's your last name?"

"Iscariot."

"Iscariot? You mean, like–"

"Judas."

"Yes! Don't worry, I'm sure you aren't like Judas."

"Like Judas? Actually, he was–"

I stop myself. I don't need to explain anything.

"Never mind," I say. I try to get past her, but she starts talking again.

"I saw you with your car, is that yours?"

Who else's would it be? "Yep."

"It's quite vintage, isn't it? What year is it?"

"'65."

"1965! Oh my, that is quite old."

"It is."

"Yes, well, I'm just off to the pharmacist. It is open late, isn't it?"

I shrug. Look at my door again. How I wish I could get to it.

"Well, my daughter is quite sick, you see. I need to get her medication, or we won't be getting any sleep tonight."

I stare at her flat. The feeling returns, and I'm tempted to say that her daughter is not sick. That she's far from sick. That it's what's inside of her that is sick, and no amount of antidepressants or placebos will calm her down. If anything, my experience has shown that what doctors prescribe only makes it worse.

But I don't.

Because it's not my problem, and I don't need to make it my problem.

"Her name is Evie, by the way," Grace tells me.

"Huh?"

"My daughter. She's Evie. She's sixteen, goes to the local comprehensive. Doesn't have many friends, but she's a lovely girl, she really is."

I wonder why this woman is telling me all this, then it strikes me just how lonely she must be. I've never seen another soul enter or leave her house. She's a single mother with a sick daughter. Probably doesn't get many people to talk to, so she emotionally unloads onto the first person she meets.

I'd feel sorry for her if I wasn't already using up all my *sorry* on myself.

"So, where do you come from?" she asks.

I shrug. "Around."

"Well, if you ever need any neighbourly favours, let me know. I make a wonderful cup of tea, and I pop down to the shops most days."

I force a smile and use the gap in conversation to get past her.

I reach my door, and out of the corner of my eye, I see her go to speak again. But she doesn't. And she leaves. Finally. And I enter my dingy, pathetic flat—wondering how, in Grace's home, two people share such a small space—and I lock and bolt the door behind me.

I overcook the pulled pork as I fall asleep on the sofa. I scrape it from the oven dish onto a roll that's only slightly hard. I pour myself an ale and delight at the first sip against a parched throat. I watch a quiz show, then flick through channels until it's dark outside and the replays of television programs with sign language interpreters have started.

That's when I know it's time to go to bed—when the person at the bottom of the screen appears, waving their hands in a way that I'm sure makes sense to someone.

I turn the television off. Listen to the silence, which is interrupted by cocky laughter from the benches outside. I ignore it and pretend that I live in a nice place.

I undress. Squeeze the last bit of toothpaste onto my toothbrush and spend a minimal amount of time brushing my teeth. Have a quick wash. Have a piss. Then climb into bed, sighing as another pointless day ends.

There are books on my bedside table with broken spines and faded pages. I found them in a charity shop. I don't feel like reading any of them.

So I lay here and close my eyes, willing the bad thoughts away, and I am just drifting off when it starts.

At first, the wall shakes. Like something is pounding

against it from the other side. Then it shakes again, and my book falls off my bedside table.

Then I hear the noises.

Shrieks and screeches and moans and screams. Multiple voices entwined in one deafening roar. Over and over. Followed by another shake of the wall and clouds of dust from the bookshelves.

I know what it is.

I know exactly what it is.

It is that woman's daughter. Grace said her name was Evie. Every day I walk past that flat, and every day I feel it.

And now I can hear it.

It doesn't stop. And I don't complain like others might, because there's nothing Grace nor the council could do to stop this girl's pain.

I've heard these kinds of screams many times. Usually from a girl or boy or woman or man in the throes of possession, after the demon has taken their body and begun torturing them, forcing their victim to make unbearable noises just because it hurts the person they have chosen to torment.

No one knows why they choose their victim, they just do. I've encountered both despicable bastards and the purest of souls enduring this affliction. Even so, it seems that demons have a particular penchant for vulnerable young girls.

The wall vibrates again, and it feels like it's made of cardboard and she will burst through it at any moment.

I could do something.

I could.

But I can't.

I'm a Sensitive by name, not by permission. It wouldn't be sanctioned. It is not my responsibility.

I am not a hero.

I am not Oscar.

I could call April, but that would give away where I am.

I don't want her to know. I don't want her to be disappointed with what I'm doing with my life.

So I close my eyes. I can't tune it out, but I can get used to it. Almost. Just so long as I ignore the images it conjures. The faces of those I have encountered in similar torment, marked and wounded, pale and in pain.

Every face I've saved was exactly the same.

Then, of course, there is the girl I didn't save. The one who killed her parents. She made these noises as well. She made them for a long time before we intervened.

By then, it was too late.

But this is not my problem.

It's not my fault I know what's going on.

I just can't do it again.

I can't watch another murder get covered up because the world won't believe what happened.

So I keep my eyes shut. I put the radio on. Listen to the dulcet tones of the late-night DJ and focus on that rather than the screaming.

After a while it stops, and I manage to fall asleep.

EVIE SPEAKS

I don't know what I'm doing.

It's like I'm walking around in a daze. I'm there, but I'm not. It's fuzzy like I'm tired, but I get eight hours sleep a night just like the books say I'm supposed to.

In English, we are asked to write a story. One about our happiest memory. It is a creative writing exercise, and we are supposed to use a wide vocabulary and lots of similes and metaphors—Miss Charlie says that's what will get us marks in our GCSE exam. She says it isn't about writing something wonderful; it's about writing something that ticks all the boxes. I don't know what that means, but I write the story anyway, as I'm excited to share this memory.

I open my purple, fluffy pencil case, and take out my pen that has a picture of Belle dancing with The Beast on it. It's blue, and I always prefer to write in blue. It's neater. Black just merges with the lines. Blue looks professional.

I start writing. I tell the story about when I was seven and Mummy and I went to Cotswold Wildlife Park. I was most excited to see the meerkats, as I like how they are always standing on guard, like sentries, or like those guards outside

Buckingham Palace. They always hold their paws in front of them, like the brown tabby cat that lives on our estate does when she tries to peer through windows. I always put my arm out so the cat can rest its paws on my arm, and not have to worry about falling over.

We saw a lot of animals that day. The rhinos, the giraffes, even the lions. They had a small enclosure with snakes, which I do not like—but I was brave, and I went in and saw them on the other side of the glass, pleased that they couldn't get to me. They were more docile than I was expecting. I thought they'd be looking at me or wriggling around, but they barely moved. Then again, there wasn't much room for them to move in the small tank they were kept in.

Mummy said she'd buy me an ice cream. It was a sunny day, and the queue was long, but I really wanted one, so we waited. And we waited. And we waited. So long that Mummy made me reapply my suntan lotion. It smelt like coconut, and I liked the idea that it would make my arms and legs and face smell like coconut too.

When we finally reached the front of the queue, Mummy bought me ice cream in a cone with a chocolate flake. The ice cream was really tall and went high into the sky, and I licked it on one side, then the other, wanting to make sure I didn't push it too far in case it fell off the cone.

We carried on walking, and we went past the meerkats, and I got excited, so excited that my arms waved, and the ice cream leant to the side and the ice cream did fall out of the cone. I remember crying and Mummy telling me not to cry so loudly because people were looking. I didn't care. I really wanted that ice cream and I really wanted to see the meerkats and the whole day was ruined.

Then this man walked past with olive skin and a kind smile. He'd just bought an ice cream, and he crouched down to me, and he said, "Did you just drop your ice cream?"

I rubbed my eyes and nodded.

"Well, here, you can have mine."

"Oh really, that's not necessary," Mummy said.

"Really, I haven't even taken a lick yet. I just bought it. It's yours."

"Really?" I asked.

"Really."

I took the ice cream. This one had strawberry sauce on it, and I hadn't thought to ask for strawberry sauce. It was sweet and made the ice cream even better.

Mummy thanked the man, and I sat on a bench, careful not to walk around with it, as I did not want to lose this one as well.

I saw that man again a few times in the following weeks. Mummy spoke on the phone to him, and he came to stay over at our house, then I never saw him again, and it was like he'd never entered our life. But I didn't care. I just remember how much I loved strawberry sauce on my ice cream, and I have always asked for strawberry sauce ever since.

I glance at the clock. It's been half an hour and I've been writing solidly all this time, and my wrist is hurting. I tried to include lots of good adjectives like Miss said we should, like the word *devastated* to describe how I felt when I dropped the ice cream, and *elated* to describe how I felt when I had a new one.

I write the last full stop and let my wrist rest. I smile, pleased with what I've done, and I go to read it back.

Only when I do, I don't see a single word of my story.

I've written four pages, back and front, but there is not a single mention of ice creams or meerkats or the nice man.

It is just the same line, over and over:

she killed her baby
she killed her baby
she killed her baby
she killed her baby

I drop my pen. Push my chair away from the desk.

What on earth is this?

This isn't my story. This isn't what I wrote.

But it's my handwriting.

I don't understand. Who killed whose baby?

I look around. Check no one has seen this. I cover the book with my arms and try to hide the shame on my face. A group of girls sit cross-legged on the table next to mine. Their skirts ride up their thighs and they laugh and chew gum with their mouths open. A few of the smart kids are still writing. A few boys are starting to arm wrestle.

No one looks in my direction.

"Right then," announces Miss Charlie. "I think most of us are done, so if you're still writing, just finish off."

I look at Miss. There's something odd about her. Something peculiar.

And I see it.

I don't know how I see it, but I see it.

A glimpse of her past.

She lies on a hospital bed. She's a teenager. They've given her a local anaesthetic to numb the cervix, but I don't know what those words mean.

She spreads her legs.

She tries not to cry.

They move a tube toward her vagina. There's something that looks like a plunger at the end of it. They place it inside of her and my body tenses and I feel sick. It moves further inside her, and the doctor tells her they are about to start the suction.

The next thing I know, she's sitting in a small room, and she's crying. Her mother sits next to her. She tells her she did the right thing. Miss Charlie cries, saliva hangs from her braces, and she covers an acne-ridden face.

She thought he loved her.

She was wrong.

"Right then, put your pens down, please."

I look at her now. Her skin is clearer. Her teeth are straighter. But it was her. Without a doubt.

"Would anyone like to volunteer to read an extract from what they've written?"

My hand fires up.

"Evie, lovely, thank you."

I'm shocked when she asks me. I look at my raised arm. I don't know why I raised it.

And I don't know why I stare so intently at this teacher, with a classroom full of silent students staring at me, ready to hear a story they can mock later; but I don't read out my story—I just ask her a very simple question.

"Why did you kill your baby?"

Miss Charlie frowns. The class look from me to her. Mouths hang open. My teacher stutters over words, not sure what to say.

"Evie, I–"

"I know you were young, but you murdered it. Why would you do that?"

I don't know why I'm asking this.

I hear the words. I know it's my voice. I know I'm saying it, that I'm asking it, but I don't know why I'm asking it. It just comes out. Like vomit, I feel it in my stomach, then I can't control it lurching up through my throat and spewing out of my mouth.

"Evie, I…"

I look at her expectantly. I blink. Everyone stares.

They always stare.

"You need to pack up your things and go to isolation."

I don't move.

"Now!"

Suddenly, I am aware. I know what I've said. I don't know why I've said it.

I stand. Place my pen back in my pencil case. Close my exercise book. Place them both in my bag. Place my bag over my shoulder. Shuffle past the rows of students. I have to ask one of them to move. Someone mutters "tramp" as I pass them.

As soon as I am out of the classroom, I cry. Weeping into my hands. Why did I say that?

I walk through the corridors. Pictures of artwork by students that left school years ago hang on the walls. The plaster crumbles. I pass the toilets and they smell like wee.

"Evie?"

It's a man's voice.

I turn around. It's my tutor. I know his name, but I can't remember it.

"What are you doing out of class?"

I march up to him. Glaring. Not in control.

"Evie?"

I reach my hand out and I grab it. The whole thing in my hand. It's not big. I feel it between my fingers, and I squeeze it, and I squeeze it more as it gets harder.

"Evie, what the hell are you doing?"

I look him in the eyes. I see what he's done with this. I see how the woman felt afterwards. He knew she didn't say yes, but he got away with it by claiming she had never said no.

"Evie, get off!"

He gets even harder. He may argue, but he enjoys it.

"Evie!"

He tries pushing me, but I only squeeze more.

I move my face closer to his, and I feel the demented look on my face stiffen, and I say, in a voice that isn't mine, "Next time leave the fucking woman alone."

And I let go. I turn away. And I march.

I know what I saw.

I saw his sin.

I see everyone's sin.

I walk past another student, and I see him screaming at his sister. I walk past the headmistress, and I see her as a child, pushing another girl into mud. I walk past a cleaner, and I see her teenage self stealing cigarettes from her mother's purse.

I don't know why I see these things.

So I shut my eyes. Crawl into a ball in the corner of the corridor. I hear people talking to me. They say my name, over and over, but I cover my ears and tighten my eyelids and hope that, if I never see anyone or hear anyone, I don't have to see what they've done.

What happens next happens in glimpses.

Mummy sits in an office. Teachers talk to her. They say words like *concerned* and *inappropriate* and *mental health*.

The next time I am fully aware Mummy is next to me, and we're walking home. She has her arm around me. I don't know how I got here, but I'm glad she's walking me home.

Mummy tells me I'm not allowed to go back to school for two weeks. That I have to stay home with her.

I hope I never have to go back.

They are all full of sin, and they deserve to fucking die.

And…

I don't know why I just said that.

I'm sorry.

Six

I force myself out of bed for the sole reason that I'm out of alcohol. My head is pounding, and my stomach feels acidic. I hate that feeling. I take the last stale roll and eat it plain, hoping that by putting something in my belly, the feeling will go away.

In searching for my wallet, I find a watch I used to wear a few years ago in my bedside drawer. It's silver, and a woman bought it for me, though I can't remember which one. It's a nice watch. I try putting it on, but it's too tight on my wrist. You know you have problems when even your wrists are putting on weight.

I get dressed and stumble out of my door. Squint at the vague sunlight that pushes through clouds on a cold winter's morning. The lock grinds as I turn the key.

I walk quickly past next door, ignoring the feeling that just makes me feel sicker, and make my way to the stairs. The patter of my feet on the stone steps cuts through the silence. There's more graffiti on the wall. Someone has written, *I only can't see if I close my eyes.* I try to figure out what it means. It sounds like it should be deep, but honestly makes no sense.

Shaking my head to myself, I walk across the green. A few empty beer cans and spliff ends surround the base of a bench. A used condom hangs half off the base of a bin that's not even half full. I don't understand these people.

As I make my way around the corner and toward the off license, I put my hands in my pockets and keep my head down. I've learnt not to make eye contact with anyone on this estate. If you do, you either get a glare or a "what the fuck you looking at?" It's best just to keep myself to myself.

"Hi, Amanpreet," I say as a *ding* above the door announces my entry to his shop.

"Good morning," he replies. His beard is longer. He still wears his turban despite the abuse that is often graffitied on the windows of his shop, or the egg stains that are often left on it. It's something I really admire about him. He is impervious to such abuse.

Either that, or he's just used to it.

"And how are you today?"

"Not bad, Amanpreet," I say, knowing he'd rather hear something nice than the truth. "How are you?"

"Very well, thank you. Very well indeed."

I turn the corner to the alcohol aisle. There's a bottle of port on offer. I take that, along with a six-pack of lager, and place it on the counter.

"How's the wife?"

"Ah, she is very good, thank you. She is staying with her sister."

"Not causing trouble, I hope?"

"Well, I can never be sure of that."

I place a crumpled twenty-pound note on the counter. He gives me a few coins in return, and I stuff them in my pocket. With a smile and a nod, I bid farewell to Amanpreet and leave the shop.

When I return to the green, they are back. Six of them.

Some sat on the bench, smoking, and some standing. Grey tracksuit bottoms on most, black on one. One of them has a crucifix tattooed beside his eye. Each of them holds a beer. It's just gone ten in the morning.

A woman walks past. Large hoop earrings. Leather skirt. A vest with cleavage I bet she regrets.

"All right, love!" one of them shouts.

"Want to hang out with us?" asks another.

She frowns and walks on, covering her chest.

"Do you shave?" another asks, and they all crack up as she turns the corner.

I have to pass them to get home. I have no choice. So I put my head down and walk quickly, hoping they leave me alone.

They don't.

"All right, mate?" one of them asks. It doesn't sound friendly.

I ignore them. Keep walking.

"Want a beer? Maybe a spliff?"

Again, the words don't sound as friendly as they seem. It sounds mocking. Sinister.

"Oi, he's talking to you!"

I keep walking. Then a crumpled beer can hits my head, and I have to stop and turn to them.

"Woah!" they say, feigning fear at the look on my face.

"He looks like my bird when she's pissed."

They crack up.

"We asked if you wanted a beer."

"No, thank you," I unwillingly reply, enunciating each syllable. Only confidence works against these scumbags. I don't give in to the temptation to ask if they were the ones who graffitied on my car. I know they were. And I'd love to charge up to them and swing my fists, but I would be ridiculously outnumbered.

I just want a quiet life.

"Why are you always alone?" one of them asks.

"I like it alone."

"Why, so you can watch kiddie porn?"

I scowl. "Why don't you give it a rest?"

I turn and continue walking to the stairs.

"You're a fucking paedo, ain't yuh?"

"You stay away from my fucking kids!"

"Fucking wanker."

This is the intellect I'm dealing with. A man wants to be left alone, so they deduce that he's paedophile. It makes me wonder how evolution hasn't killed them off.

I return home, rushing past next door, and lock and bolt the door behind me. It's too early for a beer, so I convince myself it's not as bad to have a small glass of port instead. I settle in front of the television and wonder what I'm going to do with my life.

Do I get a job?

Doing what?

Do I want to be stuck on this estate for the rest of my life?

I bow my head. Run my hand through my hair.

Maybe I should just give up.

I've tried everything. Careers. Relationships. Friendships.

None of it worked out.

Maybe life just isn't for me.

Honestly, if I was to hang myself now, no one would notice until the flat started smelling. Even then, it wouldn't make much difference to the aroma of the estate. I'd be rotten and covered in flies by the time someone found me.

I sigh. Fuck waiting. I'm having a beer.

Within two hours I've fallen asleep in a drunken stupor.

By the time I wake up, it's dark again. The evening news is on. I've wasted the entire day.

I look in the fridge. There is a carton of milk two days past its expiry date. A rotten onion. Half an unfinished jar of pesto from a few months ago. Nothing for me to eat.

I search my pockets. I have a little cash left. Maybe I'll have some money in my bank account.

I put on my coat, hoping that my card won't get declined at the supermarket.

As I approach the door, I smell something. It smells like shit.

I open the door, and the smell overwhelms me, and I can see why. Numerous green and black bags are spread across the exterior of my flat, each containing dog shit. I look further up the corridor and I can see an empty bin lying on its side, its contents discarded in front of my home.

I bow my head. Close my eyes. Pretend I'm somewhere else.

I can't live like this.

I can't even be left alone.

With a sigh, I march to the bin, pick it up, and march back. I see Grace's face at the window to her flat. As I go to my knees and start scooping the bags back into the bin, she opens her door and pokes her head out.

"Are you okay?" she asks.

I ignore her.

She steps out of her flat and approaches me.

"Would you like some help?" she says.

"I'm fine."

"Those nasty boys! Here, let me help you–"

"I said I'm fine!"

She steps back. I know I snapped. I know she's upset. I do not care. I want to be left alone, by her and everyone else.

I hate these fuckers who think it's funny to leave piles of dog shit outside my door.

I hate this woman who thinks I need help.

But most of all, I hate myself for being the kind of man who clears it up, like it's all okay.

I wish I didn't have to endure this.

Once, I was a soldier in the war against Hell. Now I'm on my knees, pushing bags of faeces into a bin whilst my annoying neighbour watches.

I stride down the corridor to return the bin to its correct place, grumbling.

When I pass the group of lads on the green, I hear them laughing. I just walk faster.

Seven

I spend the next day with the car. With Dad. Polishing the surface that was previously graffitied over. After a while, the paint doesn't look quite as marked, and I start feeling better.

I open the hood. Check the oil. The engine coolant. I never drive the car, so these things never go down. It's just a habit. Part of a routine I've established where I check the car is healthy, even though it's never used.

Finally, I tidy the inside of the boot. There's a bottle of screen wash laid on its side, and I move it into its rightful place in the corner. Straighten up the box of cassette tapes. Whenever we'd go on a ride, Dad would tell me to choose a tape from this box to listen to, and I would rush, full of excitement, to this box, and go through them all until Dad said we were running out of time and needed to go. Then I'd just pick one at random. It didn't matter which one it was, Dad could sing along to it anyway.

Only now, as I peer into the box, it seems darker. Dust coats the cassette cases. A few are cracked. A few cases are even empty, the tapes having disappeared long ago.

I close the boot. Walk to the passenger side. Step in, sit down, and recline the seat, but only slightly. I used to recline it as far as I could go, and Dad would say if I go any further I'd end up in Hell.

I look to the driver's seat, and I see him. Stubble on his cheeks that would prick my skin those few times he actually hugged me. A kind smile that masks the rage inside. He looks at me, ignoring the bruises beneath my sleeve that were caused by his fist, and I feel normal again. Like a regular kid. With a normal dad.

We drive away, and the clanking of bottles comes from a bag on the backseat. He can't pitch a note, but he sings along to Always on My Mind without missing a word. I wonder if he's singing it for me. As he joins in with Elvis saying, *I guess I never told you I'm so happy that you're mine*, I wonder if those words are an apology.

But they aren't.

It's just words.

And it's just a song.

And when Jailhouse Rock starts, he sings along to that too.

And in my mind, I separate this Dad from the other Dad. They are two different people. This one is kind and nurturing. He takes time to care for me. He drives me around in his prized possession, singing with me, and when the cassette tape ends, he tells me stories of the things he used to do with this car. That he would swing it around country roads. That he would cruise around his hometown, grinning at everyone who couldn't afford cars like this. That he met my mother in this car.

And then his face would drop. He mentions the M word, and everything becomes tense. I can feel it in my muscles. The hairs on my arms stick on end. He turns the cassette tape over, but he doesn't sing along anymore.

He once told me I was the cancer that grew inside my mother's belly, and they should have cut me out sooner.

He told me he loved her more than a husband normally loves a wife. That he wasn't settling, that he wasn't forcing affection, and that she was perfect.

And I ruined it.

And now we drive home in silence. When we arrive, he steps out of the car and waits for me to do the same so he can lock it. He charges up the garden path, not looking back to see me trailing behind. He leaves the front door open for me but doesn't check that I follow him in. He runs upstairs, shuts the bedroom door, and I find myself some dinner.

I never minded so much when he shut himself in his bedroom. It was far better than the alternative; than the screaming. So loud his voice would crack, his fists swinging, his hands grabbing me.

When it was night-time, and there were no more noises from outside, I'd go to Dad's room, and I'd nudge the door open. He'd be laid on the bed, sleeping. I'd tiptoe to the edge of the bed. Undo the laces on his shoes and take them off. Pull the duvet back and put it over him, then make sure his alarm clock is set to wake him up for work in the morning.

Then I'd go to bed myself, and imagine whether my mother would have tucked me in the same way, had I not killed her.

But that was long ago.

And really, I'm sat in a car, staring at an empty seat, just because it's where a few good memories took place.

But when good memories are hard to find, you cling to the few you have.

Sometimes, I think of what Dad was like, and it's hard to imagine him being that man who killed himself. Then, at other times, I think of what he was like, and it surprises me he didn't do it sooner.

With a sigh, I step out of the car. Lock it. Put my hands in my pockets and trudge toward home. And I see them standing there.

The group of lads. In the corner of the car park.

Were they watching me?

They all snigger.

I stop. Glare at each of them. I'm outnumbered, but I don't give a shit anymore.

"Why did you do that?" I say, but my voice is too quiet.

"What's that, bruv?" one of them says, turning back to his friend and cackling.

"Why did you leave dog shit outside my door?"

"Don't know what you're talking about, fam." "Yeah, that weren't us." "Didn't do nothing with no dog shit, mate."

More cackling. Like a bunch of demented hyenas. Encouraging each other.

I'm accomplishing nothing by standing here, so I walk on.

"Dickheads," I mutter as I pass them.

"What's that?" "Eh, what did you say?" "We're fucking talking to you, bruv?"

I pause. Turn back to them. Their muscles bulge. They are young and full of aggression. I am older and full of fatigue.

"Nothing," I say.

"That's what I thought."

I walk away, ignoring the sniggers. By the time I reach the stairs, I can no longer hear anything but the gentle echo of my feet on the stone steps. I pass the flat that makes me feel queasy and enter mine.

There's a pile of washing-up in the sink. I should probably do it. I don't want to. But I am living in squalor. Maybe I should change that.

With a grumble, I pour washing-up liquid and hot water into the bowl, and I wipe down the plates. Sauce and bits of food are stuck to the surface, and it takes a lot of scrubbing with a scouring pad.

As I finish the last dish, I pause. I smell smoke. Is it coming from inside the house?

I walk into the narrow hallway, seeing if it gets stronger.

It doesn't. It must be coming from outside.

Is someone's house on fire?

I rush to the window. I can't see anything. I open the front door and step outside. The smell gets stronger.

I check the flat next door. It's not them.

I look down on the green. The group of lads look at me and points. And laugh. And high five.

What have they done?

I rush to the stairs, and the smell gets even stronger. I run down them, worried that someone might be in danger, and the scent becomes overwhelming as I approach the car park.

As I enter the car park, I don't quite believe it.

I fall to my knees, the gravel ripping my trousers.

I fight tears from my eyes, but I lose the battle.

"No..."

Dad's car.

It's on fire.

Not just a little—the interior is full of flames, twisting and contorting and flickering and raging. The passenger window is smashed and from inside, the fire destroys everything.

"Dad..."

Something explodes, and the engine goes up in flames too. Then it explodes again, and the fire spreads to the outside of the car.

The smoke reaches out for me and chokes me. Tightens my throat and I am suffocating.

People gather behind me. I hear shouting. Someone's calling 999. Someone's telling their kid to keep away. Someone's putting their hand on my back and I'm punching it away. Shortly after, the fire engine arrives, and they begin their fight with the most destructive of the elements.

I see Dad, on his knees, in front of the car, much like I am, crying over it. The car he met my mother in. The car where kindness prevailed.

Ruined.

And I am filled with an anger I can no longer contain.

EIGHT

I charge forward. My mind is absent. Animal instinct takes over. My feet pound the ground, and I feel my arms shaking, and I know the dire consequences of what I'm about to do, but I don't care.

I truly do not care.

Everyone has their breaking point, and once you reach it, rationality is no longer a concern.

"Oi!" I shout as soon as I see them. Six of them stood around the bench, crumpled beer cans at their feet.

I can smell the body odour and cheap deodorant from here.

"I said oi!"

They turn and look at me. Nudge each other. Snigger. Mock me.

They always fucking mock me.

What, I'm on my own? I don't want to be part of your crew? I want to keep myself to myself? To hell with these pricks.

"Look at this guy!" one says, the pitch of his voice rising

higher as he bends over to cope with the strength of his laughter.

A part of me tells me to stop. The other part of me knocks away such thoughts and replaces them with the image of Dad's car reduced to nothing but flames.

It was the only thing I had of him.

It was the only happy memory I held.

It was the only way I could convince myself that there were at least a few fleeting moments of contentment in my otherwise miserable childhood.

And these imbeciles took it from me.

I can still smell the smoke. Still sense the crowd growing. More sirens come—more fire engines to help, more police to investigate.

I won't talk to the police.

Instead, I'll deal with these bastards the way I would have dealt with them when I was a teenager.

"Yo, what you doing, cracker?"

I set my eyes on the closest one. A six-foot-five guy who seems to think he's black. He talks like black guys do in American movies, like this makes him cool.

I fucking hate this guy.

"Yo, mate, you better–"

I hold my arm back to get big a swing and I launch my fist forward until my knuckles collide with his nose. He stumbles back and he bends over and I don't relent.

Not yet. Not while he's stumbling.

I swing a fist downwards at the back of his head, forcing him to his knees.

Another approaches. A skinhead wearing a vest. I hate vests. No man ever looks good in a vest unless they have muscles, and this prick has two spindly arms dangling like cheese strings.

He throws a punch. I dodge it. I swing an uppercut at the underside of his chin.

The rest approach. I am outnumbered. The element of surprise that allowed me a few punches has gone. So I just charge at them and swing my arms, sending my fists whichever way they will go.

This lasts only a few seconds until one of them winds me with a hard punch to the chest. I wheeze, trying to make sure I can still breathe, and another one impacts my cheek with a hard punch.

I stumble back. My cheekbone throbs. A fist on the back of my head makes everything go fuzzy and the next thing I know, I am on the floor, and they are kicking my shins, my knee, my face, my chest. They stomp on my neck and crotch. All of them. It's relentless. And I can do nothing but writhe around on the floor and endure the pain.

I can see Dad's face.

"Stop being such a wimp. You disappoint me."

I'm sorry, Dad.

After a while, I get used to the pain. It's constant, and every part of my body aches, but the strikes to my skull make it all a little more distant.

Then, through the haze, I hear a woman's voice. I don't know what she's saying. She's shouting. I think I catch something like *leave him alone* and *get off him*.

The next thing I know, I'm laid on my back, and they aren't kicking me anymore. The clouds move slowly across my vision. The sky is overcast, and I'm fairly sure a raincloud is approaching.

There is a hand on my neck. But a nice hand. Two fingers pressing against my throat to check my pulse.

My head tilts to the side, and her face comes into focus.

Grace. My next-door neighbour.

"Come on," she says. "Let's get you to your feet."

She helps me lean up. I taste blood. Her hand on my back feels comforting.

"That's it, in your own time."

Then she places an arm around me and guides me to my feet. I try walking and a pain shoots up and down my leg. My knee feels weak as I put pressure on my it.

"Come on, let's get you to my flat."

To her flat? No, I can't do that. I don't want to be involved. I want to be left alone.

"I'll... be fine... in my own..."

"Don't be silly—I used to be a nurse. Unless you want to go to the hospital?"

"No. God, no. No hospitals."

"Right, well I'm the next best thing."

I shake my head and grumble. We reach the first step and I grip the banister and wince as I lift my leg to the second step.

"Really, I will be fine."

"No, you will not be fine. I'm not going to argue with you —you are coming to my home so I can help you."

"But–"

"No buts. You could be concussed, and it is not safe for you to go back to your flat on your own."

I go to open my mouth again, but I don't have the energy to argue with her.

We make it up a few more steps, slowly, every movement of muscle prompting another burst of pain. Her hand on my back is comforting. It feels nurturing. I imagine it's how it might feel to have a mother.

Eventually, we make it to the top step, and I have to pause. Gather my breath. I go to argue about going to her flat again, then she drags me forward, and the words die in my throat. She opens the door to her home and helps me limp inside.

It's dark. Even with the lights on, it's dark. Unopened mail sits in the corner of the hallway. The wallpaper is outdated and peeling off. It smells stale.

I recognise the smell.

It's the smell of evil.

She helps me through the hallway, past the kitchen where dirty pots and pans remain untouched, and to her living room, where she sits me on a sofa. I can feel the springs pressing against my buttocks. The window has been blacked out with large sheets of card with duct tape around the edges.

She leaves me for a moment, then returns with a first aid kit. She kneels down and begins on my face. I flinch as a cotton bud meets my cheek. She dabs it and I see blood on it. I didn't even realise my face was bleeding.

"Why is the light blocked out?"

"Oh, that's for my daughter."

"What, she doesn't like to look outside?"

"No, she has photophobia. She finds the light uncomfortable. It's too bright. We used to have curtains, but light still shone through, and she found it too much, so we just ended up blocking it out."

I sigh. Her daughter doesn't have photophobia.

She doesn't have a clue what's happening to her daughter.

She takes some cream and rubs it against my cheek.

"You're going to have a black eye," she tells me. "It's swelling, and it's already darkened."

"I'll have to call off the beauty pageant then."

She laughs.

It feels good making someone laugh.

She lifts my trouser leg and feels my calf and my knee. I know she's checking for injuries, but I can't help but feel uncomfortable. Her bare hands are on my skin. It's not something I'm used to.

I look around the room to distract myself. I notice a crucifix on the wall. It's upside down.

"What's with the crucifix?"

She glances over her shoulder and tuts. "Dammit, I thought I got all of them."

"What do you mean?"

"We used to have quite a few, but they just kept hanging upside down. Every single one I put up just turned the other way. In the end, I took them down. I must have missed that one."

As if on cue, a deep-throated murmur comes from a bedroom.

"That your daughter?"

"Yes, her name is Evie. She's ill, and she sometimes makes those noises."

She wraps a bandage around my knee.

"What's Evie like with religious artefacts?"

"She hates them. I don't know why. I raised her to be a good Catholic girl, and she always has been. Only now..."

I nod. She doesn't look up. I can sense the tears in her eyes that she's trying not to let me see. The last thing she wants is to cry in front of me.

It's a pain I've seen in many mothers.

"What's her diagnosis? I mean, if you don't mind me asking."

"Well, it depends which doctor you listen to, as we've been to so many. One says paranoid schizophrenic, another says psychosis. Another says she's just a teenage girl playing up."

"And what's she like at school?"

"She doesn't go to school."

"You home school her?"

"No. She's been suspended, pending investigation. I... Sorry, I..."

"It's okay. I'm being intrusive. I'll stop."

"No, it's not that. It's just..."

I place a hand on her shoulder and tell her, "It's fine. I'm asking too many questions."

She tends to the rest of my wounds in silence. Sometimes, another grumble comes from the bedroom, but Grace doesn't react. Like she's used to it. It's not a natural noise for a teenage girl to make, but it's so much a part of Grace's life that it doesn't even make her flinch.

When she's done, I thank her, and I push myself up.

"Are you sure you wouldn't like a cup of tea or anything?"

"No, thank you. I best get back."

I don't think of an excuse to leave, but this time, she doesn't argue.

"Thank you for your help."

"You're welcome."

My bones feel stuff. My muscles ache. The bandage around my knee forces me to straighten my leg. But I feel better, if only because of the care she's given to me.

As I open the door to leave, I turn back and give her a smile. I try to make it look genuine, but I don't think anyone would buy it.

"I hope your daughter gets better," I tell her, knowing full well that she will not.

"Thank you," she says, and shuts the door, and I can finally return to my flat.

Nine

I close my eyes, and it starts again. As the darkness of the night grows more intense, so does the girl's torment.

I lay in bed, listening to the screams. Over and over. She's inches away, on the other side of the wall, but it feels like she's right beside me, roaring into my ear.

Sometimes there are words. Most are unintelligible, but I recognise some of them. I can even identify the languages.

"Sus deformem... Sus deformem..." Latin.

"Hadhih alfataat satamut... Hadhih alfataat satamut..." Arabic.

"Mrtyu... Mrtyu..." Sanskrit.

Most of the time there aren't any words. It's just a stretched, distorted cry.

The girl is in pain.

But what would you have me do?

It is not my job anymore. Nor my duty. Nor my responsibility.

I am not a Sensitive any longer. This isn't my domain.

I just need to block it out.

But my head is pounding, and it's impossible to block it out; each scream feels like a hammer to my skull.

Why did this girl have to be in the flat beside mine?

There are at least a hundred flats in this block, and there are at least thirty council flat blocks in this county alone.

Why did I have to be assigned the one flat where the girl on the other side of the wall is having a full-blown demonic episode?

Maybe it's too late for her.

I know what happens when it gets too late. When the demon has taken the body for too long. When the soul is pushed out and the demon replaces it.

It's called amalgamation incarnation. It takes about a year of possession. It is the process by which the demon takes the body from its host completely, and the host is sent to Hell as the demon takes its place in this world.

It's not just the pain the girl is suffering in this life that she needs to fear—it is the eternal damnation she will suffer if there is no intervention.

But it's not up to me, dammit!

What, just because I know these things, I have a duty to help?

What would I even say to Grace?

"Oh, hey, thanks for stitching my wounds up. Mind if I exorcise your daughter?"

Then again, she seems like a devout Catholic. Maybe she'd be more on board than I think.

Or maybe I should just mind my own damn business.

I came here for solace. To be alone. To live without having to affect, or be affected by, another person.

I never intended to cause grief with the local scum. I just wanted to take care of Dad's car and enjoy the little comfort it gave me.

I checked on the car before I went to bed. It was

completely black. No colour remained. The cassette tapes were destroyed, as were the memories.

They will take the car away tomorrow. It's no use to me now, anyway. It's no longer a source of happy memories; it's another reminder of how I let Dad down, yet again.

I can see his face, his snarling grimace, telling me how I screwed up once more. Once he'd finish reprimanding me about the car, he'd list all the other times I've disappointed him—coming last on sports day, not joining the school football team, and, oh yeah, how I killed his wife before I had even been born.

Another screech builds to a crescendo, and the wall vibrates following the impact of something hard. A shelf above the bed rattles. I already removed the few books that were on there, placing my *Ars Goetia* text in the cupboard under the sink.

Another collision and the wall trembles.

I rub my head. My head is throbbing. I already took painkillers. Do I have any sleeping pills? Is it even safe for me to take sleeping pills with painkillers?

I best not, just in case.

Then again, what am I worried about? That I'd die in my sleep?

That would be a reward few get to receive.

Another scream and the wall shudders, this time for longer.

I wonder what Grace is doing while all of this is happening. Does she weep in her room with the door shut and a pillow over her head? Does she wipe her eyes and wonder what she did wrong? Does she accept she will get no sleep?

Or, is she in there right now, sat beside her daughter, with Evie's hand clutched between hers, whispering *it's going to be okay* and knowing fully well that it is not.

I turn onto my side. I sigh.

Grace helped me. She stopped the assaults against me, and she patched me up. Maybe I owe her this.

Then again, I never asked her to help me. I never asked to enter her life.

Another roar. In this one, I can hear multiple voices. They come together in a symphony of wails, producing a sound only a demon could create

I don't want to hear that sound again.

But it will go on. Night after night. And eventually it will be too late, and Evie will not be present anymore.

Maybe if I just talk to Grace... Point her in the right direction of someone who will be willing to help her...

But if the Sensitives helped, they'd find out where I am.

I shake my head. I can't believe I'm agreeing to this. I don't want to get involved.

The image of a dead girl and her slain parents presents itself to my thoughts—a constant reminder of what I have to lose.

But an eternity in Hell would be far, far worse.

Fine.

I will talk to Grace.

I will meet Evie.

But that is it.

Another rattle of the wall and another scream.

I take the duvet to the sofa, where I can still hear the shrieks, but I can at least have a hope of getting to sleep, so long as I don't think of the mother and daughter and their grave situation.

And I try not to let myself care.

EVIE SPEAKS

I wake up a few times during the night. Usually by screaming. But then I open my eyes and there's no one else here, and I wonder—was it me screaming?

Every morning as I push myself out of bed, forcing myself from a warm duvet, still so tired despite eight hours of sleep, I wipe the gunk from the corners of my eyes and reach for some water to ease the stinging in my throat.

It feels like someone has run sandpaper up the insides of my windpipe, or like it's made of gravel.

I try saying something, just a word, like *hello*, and it comes out in a hoarse whisper. I try to remember dreams, wondering if I was screaming in them, and therefore screaming in real life. I often get involved in my dreams. I woke myself up by punching the wall once, and a few weeks ago Mummy said she found me stood over her bed singing *Goosey Goosey Gander.*

I recall an image from a nightmare, one so vivid that any description I give it would not do it justice. A group of Catholic priests, hidden away in a room with no light, repeat Latin prayers. I don't know how I know it was Latin. They were in a priest hole, hiding themselves away.

Goosey Goosey Gander, whither shall I wander…

She sings it to me.

She says it's her favourite nursery rhyme.

She says it reminds her of a time when she was happy.

Upstairs and downstairs and in my lady's chamber…

The nightmare becomes clearer. The door opens. The priests turn. They don't move—they are stricken with fear, and want to run, but know it would be pointless.

They are caught.

There I met a man who wouldn't say his prayers…

They round the priests up.

Take them away.

And murder each one of them. Publicly. Labelling them as traitors.

Take him by the left leg, throw him down the stairs…

I shake my head. Run my hands over my face. Try to free myself from the thoughts.

I have these images, sometimes, of things that I couldn't possibly know, so clear that I can't tell where they came from.

Like the man next door. I saw him talking to Mummy. I also saw him as a child. His hair was scruffy, and his clothes were too big. He hid behind a door. His father burst in, stumbling from wall to wall, shouting for him, but the boy was not afraid.

But he's afraid now.

That's all I can see in him. Fear.

It smells like dead bugs and old milk.

"Evie, are you coming for breakfast?"

I turn my head slowly toward the door. *The wretch calls us.* She wants to feed us. *She wants to take me away from you, Evie.*

But it's just breakfast.

It's poisonous, don't eat it.

Mummy wouldn't poison me.

No, but she might poison me.

"Evie, did you hear me?"

"Yes, Mummy."

"I've done you an omelette."

She's put acid in it...

... or cyanide...

... or bleach...

... she's going to kill us, Evie...

... please don't let her kill us...

"I'm coming!"

I stand. Rub my eyes.

Her hands are on my shoulders, guiding me, and I'm not in control. It's like my body is a car and I'm in the backseat. I can tell where we're going, but I can only see the back of the driver's head.

I leave my room. Cardboard blocks light from the windows, and the artificial light gives the flat an unnatural glow. I run my fingers against the bumps of the wall and notice how pale my skin is. The wallpaper crumbles a little more than it did yesterday. It's a floral design that belongs in a home from the 1980s. It makes us feel sick. But the crucifix that rests upside down on the wall makes us smile.

I assume Mummy has stopped trying to take them down now. *We* like this. The longer it remains there, hanging loosely, the longer *we* mock their Saviour, and the stronger *we* grow.

I rub my eyes as I hobble through the hallway. My body aches. My muscles give a tinge of pain with every step. It feels like I've been running for hours, and every part of my body is suffering.

But I've been asleep.

I don't understand why my body hurts like this.

It doesn't matter.

What?

Just don't let her poison us.

I look at Mummy. She places an omelette on the table. It has bits of bacon and leek in. She places a glass of fresh orange juice in front of it. There is a fork and a knife. We could use them to impale her.

"Your favourite," Mummy says, beaming at me.

"What time is it?" I ask.

"It's half-past nine."

"Don't I need to be at school?"

Mummy pauses. Sighs. "Not at the moment."

"Why not?"

"School has asked if you can stay home. Just for a few days."

"Why?"

She wipes her hands on her apron and ignores the question. "I think it's a good idea. It means I can take care of you. Doesn't it?"

"Take care of me?"

"Yes, Evie. You aren't well."

I'm not well?

But we are well.

Are we?

We are perfectly well.

We are perfectly well.

But we'll be dead if you eat that poisonous omelette.

I look at the omelette. To Mummy. She smiles so widely. But it's not her real smile. It's the one she does when she's trying to make everyone happy. It's fake.

And I won't let her kill us.

"Come on, Evie, why don't you–"

I take the plate and launch it across the room. The plate shatters against the wall and its pieces fall to the floor. The omelette slides down the fading wallpaper, leaving a trail like a slug.

Mummy's smile is gone now. Her mouth is open. Wide open. She stares at us. Her hands are rigid by her side.

Another omelette sizzles on the frying pan, but she doesn't tend to it.

"Evie, I..."

We scowl. She stops talking and steps back. I don't know how my expression looks, but it's enough to make her recoil.

Slowly, she regains some composure. She turns the stove off so that the omelette stops cooking. It hasn't finished yet. Right now, it's just hot raw eggs.

"Evie, why did you do that?"

"We won't let you poison us."

"Us? What *us*? Who is *us,* Evie?"

Huh?

What?

I shake my body and I look at the smashed plate and what have I done?

Did I do that?

Oh my gosh, how could I do that?

"Mummy, I'm so sorry!"

I rush to the cupboard beneath the sink and take out a brush and dustpan, go to my knees, and make sure I get every little bit, reaching under the table and under the oven, ensuring no piece of plate is left unattended to.

When I stand, I look to Mummy, suppressing tears, and say, "I'm so sorry, I'll buy another one. I'll use my pocket money, I promise."

"Oh, Evie. You don't need to do that."

Mummy's arms wrap around me, and I feel warm and comforted and loved and complete. She sniffs my hair. Her face rests against my forehead. I think she's crying, but I'm not sure.

"What's wrong with me, Mummy?"

"I don't know, darling. You're just ill. But you will get better, you will."

She laughs.

Not Mummy; the other one in here with us.

She cackles at the suggestion.

She says we already are *better*.

That we are not sick.

That we are simply above human comprehension.

And when Mummy releases me from her arms, I feel *her* arms replace them, and they are warmer, and tighter, and more loving.

I gaze at Mummy, wishing she could understand me as well as *she* does.

It's because I love you more, Evie...

It's because she loves me more.

We are stronger than her, Evie...

We are stronger.

And I will never let us be apart...

I've never felt as loved as I do with *her*.

She says the right things at the right time.

She asks me if she could stay, and I beg her to never leave.

Mummy makes another omelette and I eat it, though we throw it up again later, all over the shoe rack. And we leave it. The bitch can deal with it.

We have better things to think about.

TEN

I spend the day watching awful television whilst trying to talk myself into knocking on next door. Politicians debate menial decisions, inbred idiots argue over who cheated on who, and a group of men cook pointless meals—and I barely watch a moment of it.

The entire time, I'm just wondering how to approach Grace, and asking myself when I became so awful at talking to people. I used to be a troubled kid, but I was an outgoing kid, never shy about showing off at a party. I'd banter with colleagues, show off in front of women, and make friends with strangers in pubs. Now, just going next door to speak to an evidently fragile woman feels like I'm leaping into a tank of sharks. I question every word I plan to say, become self-conscious of every body movement, and wonder whether I am actually doing the right thing.

Hah. 'The right thing.' There is no such thing as 'the right thing.' There are just *things*. You speak, you act, and you do—and none of it means a damn thing. Besides, what you probably consider right today, you'll be condemned for tomorrow. Like exorcisms. We have to hide it now, but I'd have been in demand a few centuries ago. I think too many of us suffer because we are born at the wrong time. There are murderers in prison who'd have made great gladiators. People locked away in asylums for hearing God talk to them who would have once been prophets. Psychopaths who would have once been the king's best assassins.

When evening arrives, I take a bottle of cheap Merlot from the shelf, leave the flat, and go to knock on Grace's door. Pause. Why am I doing this again? Do I really need to do this?

Yes. I do.

But do I?

I hesitate. Exhale a long, exasperated breath. Lean my head against the door.

Life was so much easier a few days ago, when I could keep myself to myself. I was far away from the world of the demonic. I didn't feel compelled to help the mother and daughter next door. I was content living my ignorant, stubborn life.

Before I can second-guess myself again, I swing the door open and march outside. I lock up, then take the few steps to next door. Take a moment. Then knock a few times.

Shuffling comes from inside of the house. Followed by unlocking. Then the door swings open. Grace stands there. She looks even worse. Her hair sticks up in various places, her dressing gown is tatty, and she seems to be hobbling forward.

"Hi, I, er..." I try to gather my thoughts. "My name is Mo, by the way. Short for Moses. I don't know if I mentioned that yesterday."

"I think you did. Hello, Mo."

"Hi. Look, I, erm..." I lift the bottle of wine. "I had this bottle of wine, and I was thinking, well, I don't really want to drink it alone. I was wondering whether you'd be willing to share a glass with me?"

Her eyes light up. Suddenly, her tired, pale face shows a glimpse of a smile.

"I'd love to. I mean—I don't drink. But if you'd like a glass of wine, I'm sure I can join you with a cup of tea?"

I feel suddenly stupid for bringing the bottle of wine. "Of course."

She stands back and lets me in. When she shuts the door behind me, we are in almost complete darkness. There is not a visible window left in the house.

"This way," she says, guiding me to the kitchen, where she takes a glass out of a cupboard and places it on the table. The table is a small garden table, and the chairs are wooden and look uncomfortable. The cupboard squeaks as she closes it.

She puts the kettle on for herself.

I take a seat, open the bottle, and pour myself a small glass. Then I wonder who I'm kidding and fill the glass up.

"Is Evie in at the moment?"

"Yes, she is. She's in her room. She spends most of her time in there."

I look toward Evie's room. She's unusually quiet. Maybe I'm wrong.

Then I notice the upside-down crucifix and the smell of rotten eggs, and I know I am not.

Once the kettle has boiled, Grace places a tea bag in a stained cup and pours the hot water. She opens the fridge. There are three almost empty milk cartons. She sniffs two of them and puts them back, then chooses the third.

She splashes a little milk in, then brings the mug to the table and sits opposite me.

An awkward silence settles between us, and I am keen to fill it.

"So, Grace, where do you come from?"

"Oh, I've lived here my whole life. I grew up on an estate down the road, then moved here when I had Evie."

"Are you married?"

"No. I mean, I was. He wasn't very nice in the end."She takes a sip of her tea. A flicker of pain passes over her face, but she's quick to reject it.

"I'm sorry to hear that," I tell her.

"Yes. It's been a long time now. He's no longer in our lives, so..."

I nod. Think desperately for another conversation starter.

"You said you used to be a nurse."

"Did I? Oh, yes. I did. But that was a while ago."

"What made you stop?"

"I found it difficult. They signed me off with stress one day, and, well, I guess I never went back. They told me it was postpartum depression. I've always wanted to return to it, it's just... With how things are with Evie, it's difficult."

I nod. Sip my wine. Try to think of a topic that wouldn't conjure stories of sadness. Is there nothing in this woman's life that brings her joy?

Then I figure, seeing as she's brought Evie up, this may be the best time to broach the subject.

"How is Evie doing?"

"Oh, well..." She shrugs. "You know?"

"You can be honest with me."

"I'm sure I can. Do you have children, Mo?"

"No, I do not."

"Shame. You seem like you would make a good father."

I force a smile. "What have the doctors said about her?"

"The doctors can't agree. They have said many things, yet nothing at the same time."

"I guess that's doctors for you."

"It's just... She was always such a good girl. I raised her Catholic, making sure she obeyed God's word, ensuring she understood about chastity and the correct way for a young girl to behave. I really don't understand why this happened. Why God would let..."

She trails off and stares at the floor.

"Sometimes that's exactly why," I tell her.

"What do you mean?"

"The Devil likes to mock God, and that is why he will pick His most devout children. Sometimes being better behaved makes you more susceptible to attack—a sense of irony the Devil enjoys, perhaps."

"How do you know about such things?"

I sigh. Shift in my seat. Wonder how much to tell her.

"I used to offer... spiritual counselling, shall we say. To those inflicted by ailments medicine couldn't cure. I helped those in need."

"And what did that involve?"

"Talking. Comforting. Praying."

I choose not to include *exorcism* for now. I know she's Catholic, but nowadays, that doesn't necessarily mean she believes in demons.

"Is this something you think could help Evie?"

"I don't know. Yes. No. Maybe."

"Is it something worth trying?"

I watch Grace's face. Absorb the anguish in her quivering lip, the flicker of her eyebrows, the quickness of her breath. Her arms shake, whether from insomnia or anxiety or grief, I do not know, but this is a woman who has dealt with a lot of pain.

This is a woman whose home is vulnerable, and she has no idea.

"May I meet her?" I ask.

"Evie?"

"Yes. If I could meet her, then maybe I could see if there's any help I could give her."

Her eyes float to the side, to the hallway, toward Evie's

bedroom, and they hover there. She tucks her dressing gown further around herself. She bites her lip, then looks back at me.

"She's awfully sick," she tells me.

"I understand."

"She's not in a good way. If you were to meet her, then you might question me as a mother, and I—"

"I would never question you as a mother, Grace. I think, from the look of it, you are doing all you can, and you are struggling."

Her lip shakes. I can see her trying to hold back tears. "I am struggling. I really am. The school won't even take her back. Now she's at home. With me. All day. And I don't know what to do..."

She breaks. Her head drops. Tears trickle down her cheeks. I move my chair around the table until I'm beside her and place a hand on her back. I remember doing this with April, too, when she was in pain. There is no cure for heartbreak, and a hand on the back seems pitiful when all is considered. So I take my hand away and shuffle back to my side of the table.

Grace takes some kitchen roll and wipes her eyes.

"Sorry."

"It's fine."

"No, I mean—this is the first time I've had someone over in a long time and I end up in tears."

"I understand. It's okay."

She finishes wiping her cheeks. Her eyes are still red.

"May I see her?" I ask.

"If you're sure."

I take a deep breath. "Yes, I am."

She nods faintly, stands up, and leads me to her daughter's room.

ELEVEN

The closer we get to Evie's room, the colder the flat becomes. The hairs on my arms prick up. I can see my breath.

Grace doesn't notice. Perhaps she's used to it.

I reach the bedroom door. Evie's name is stuck to it with purple letters, though half of the V is missing, as is the E. It looks like it says Eli. I know this is intentional. Eli was mentioned in the Book of Samuel, in the Hebrew Bible. His sons violated God's wishes by eating sacrifices that were meant for Him, and had sex with women outside a place of worship —when word of their behaviour came back to Eli, he was disappointed, but he sided with his sons over God. As a punishment, God cursed Eli's house so that no one would reach old age.

Was this a message? An insult to Grace that she would not understand? An insinuation that her child will not reach old age, and that she has been irresponsible with her parenting?

Maybe. Maybe not. Demons love a mind-fuck, and that's probably all it's meant to be.

I knock gently on the door.

There is no reply, but I hear shuffling from inside.

I turn and look at Grace. "Could you make sure it's okay for me to go in?"

She nods faintly and steps forward, fiddling with the belt around her dressing gown.

"Evie?" she calls out. "Evie, darling, can we come in?"

There is no response.

"We are coming in, Evie... if that's okay."

She turns the door handle, pushes the door open, then steps back.

This poor woman is afraid of her own daughter.

I smile at her. I understand the bravery it takes for her to disturb her violent child, and how that fear is destroying he.

I step inside. There is no light, but I can make out the outline of Evie in the darkness. She sits on the floor, her back to me, scribbling something.

"Hello, Evie," I say. "My name is Moses Iscariot. Do you mind if I put a lamp on?"

She doesn't turn around. I edge toward the bedside lamp and put it on anyway. It lights half her body. Her hair is long and matted, and its greasy strands shine in response to the vague illumination.

I walk forward, slowly, and sit on the edge of the bed, a few feet from her back. Over her shoulder, I can see crayons spread over the floor, and pieces of white A4 paper. Her arm moves quickly, scribbling away.

"Your mother tells me you've been unwell, Evie," I tell her. "I think I might be able to help you."

She doesn't respond.

"Would you be okay with that? If I were to help you?"

A low-pitched croak pushes out of her mouth.

"What's that, Evie?"

It comes again, a little louder.

"I can't hear you."

"*Non opus est tibi ut beneficium...*"

It's Latin. She's saying 'we' do not need help.

The fact that she's referring to herself as 'we' suggests this thing has already made contact with her conscious self. It's made Evie aware of its presence, and has taken control of her. The difference between Evie and whatever is inside of her will be almost indistinguishable to anyone else.

I turn to Grace, who stands in the doorway, the lamplight highlighting the bags under her eyes.

"Do they teach Latin at her school?"

"Latin? No, I don't think so."

"Is there anywhere else she might have picked it up?"

"Not that I can think of."

I watch her for a moment. Her voice is so soft and weak. She is a kind woman, but I wonder how much more she can take until that changes.

I nod and turn back to Evie. I shuffle a little closer to her, so that I can see over her shoulder.

"Can I talk to Evie?"

She stops scribbling. Turns her head slightly. I can make out the tip of her nose, but her features are otherwise covered by her hair.

"And I don't mean both of you, I mean just Evie. Is she allowed to talk to me?"

"We are Evie." Her voice is croaky, cracking under the strain of many nights of constant screaming.

"Well, that's not possible, is it? It's either *I* am Evie, or *we* are Evie and... whoever else is there."

She lets out a long, murmuring growl, then adds, "*We* are Evie," and turns back to the drawings.

"Okay, if you say so. So what is it you've been drawing?"

"We've been making pictures."

"What kind of pictures?"

"Nice, lovely pictures."

"Can I see one?"

She reaches for a sheet of paper and lifts it. It is of a single flower, with a green stem and blood red petals. There are a few scribbles outside of the line, but it's coloured in well.

"That's a very nice picture, Evie."

She shakes her head; slow but large rotations from side to side. "No, it's not."

"Oh? How come?"

"Because the petals are poisonous. All the bees are going to try to pollinate it, and it's just going to fill their bodies with toxicity, and they will flop, and fall to the floor, and die."

She puts the drawing down. I look over her shoulder at the other drawings. "What's that one?" I ask.

She lifts another drawing. A woman and a girl are having a picnic. They look like Grace and Evie, but healthier. There appears to be a thunderstorm and drops of dark blue fall over them.

"This one's good, too."

She hands me another one. A woman who looks identical to her mother sleeps in a bed. The wardrobe behind her is open, and a large claw reaches out from between the doors.

"These are all very good drawings, Evie."

"Would you like to see my favouritest one of all?"

"Yes, please."

She reaches under the pile of papers, moving various obscure drawings out of the way, and pulls one out. She holds it to her chest so I can't see it, then turns to me and grins. Her teeth hang over her top lip. Her skin is cracked and faded. Her eyes are fully dilated.

"What's the drawing, then?"

"I'm not sure you want to see it."

"Of course I want to see it."

Her grin widens. "Are you sure you're sure?"

"Yes, I am."

"You're not going to get mad?"

"Of course not."

"Pinkie promise?"

She holds out her pinkie finger. I hesitate to touch her, but I do it. I reach my hand out and take her pinkie in mine. Her finger is cold but sweaty. I can feel the demon glowing inside her as our skin makes contact, and I take my finger away quickly.

"Will you show me the picture now?"

She giggles and hands me the picture.

I take it. Turn it around. It is of a man with black hair and stubble on his chin, with a noose around his neck. He hangs from the ceiling. There is a red line around his throat where his neck has broken. Beside his feet is a child on his knees, head in his hands.

"Do you know who that is?" she asks.

"No, Evie, who is it?"

She smacks her forehead playfully, as if to mimic my silliness. "You really don't know?"

"I really don't. Who is it?"

"That's your daddy!"

The words don't quite register at first. They spin around my mind, echoing like we are in a chamber, until I see it.

The man looks exactly like Dad.

"And that's you!" she says, pointing to the child on the floor. "That's you upset because your daddy is dead!"

My arms shake. My fingers grip the paper hard, crumpling its sides. I don't know what to say. What to do. I try not to react, but I feel a sickness lurching up through my belly, through my throat, and it's too big to contain.

"If you'd like, I could draw a picture of your daddy as he is now."

Don't react, don't react, don't react.

It's exactly what it wants.

Don't do it.

"I could show you a picture of him being fucked by Abalam in Hell."

Her voice changes. It grows deeper. It doesn't sound natural.

"Just like Abalam will fuck April when she's down there, too."

I'm not sure what happens next. I dive forward and the next thing I know, I'm on top of her, my hands around her throat, my thumbs pressing against her windpipe, and instead of suffocating she is laughing, laughing, laughing, non-stop hysterical cackles that just won't end.

"Please!" Grace is beside me. "Please, stop!"

I squeeze harder.

"Please stop!"

It still smiles. Still laughs.

"She's ill, she doesn't know what she's saying, please just stop!"

Reality plummets back into my mind, hitting me like a sucker punch, and I back away from the girl, crawling along the floor until I reach a wall, which I rest against and let myself breathe. I'm panting. My heart is racing. And she is gazing at me, enjoying every agonising moment.

I used to be better than this.

I used to be able to control myself. Enemies will say anything to get a rise. The moment you let it get to you, you've lost your battle.

And I've lost this one before it's even begun.

I push myself up and stumble out of the room. The hallway rushes toward me, the walls narrow, and I fall to my knees at the door.

Grace is at my side, and she's speaking, and it takes a while until I can decipher the sounds she's making.

"Really, she's not well, she's a vulnerable girl, she says things to hurt us, you can't do that to her, you can't..."

I wave a hand to show I hear her. I push myself to my feet. I stumble to the front door, and put my hand on the door handle, and I don't look at her.

"I'm sorry," I say. "I shouldn't have done that. I didn't mean to hurt your daughter."

"She does these things, and she doesn't–"

"I can't help you." I close my eyes and drop my head. "I'm sorry. I thought I could, but I can't."

I swing the door open and stumble the few feet to my home. I push myself inside and bolt the door and lean against it. Panting. Weeping. Pathetic.

I'm not a warrior of Heaven.

I'm barely its slave.

I'm not even a has-been.

I'm a never-was, and the best thing I can do is leave that family alone—even if things are only going to get worse.

Far, far, far worse.

TWELVE

But I can't just leave her.

I can't.

Can I?

This isn't my business anymore.

If I were a retired police officer walking past a crime being committed, I wouldn't start chasing after the criminal, would I?

Then again, if that were the case, I might phone 999 and let them know.

So what if I find someone who *can* help Evie?

Is Evie even able to be helped anymore? Is she beyond saving?

I lean my head against the bumpy wall, feeling the indents of ageing décor against my head.

That's not my call to make. No matter how far someone is gone, you at least try.

But not me.

Not now.

Sure, I may have the ability. But I walked away from the Sensitives. It's not me anymore.

What about April?

What if I phoned April?

Told her about what was happening?

But I'd need to tell April where to go. She'd need an address. And that address is next to mine. And she'll know where I am.

Would that be a bad thing?

Of course it would.

I could leave. Go somewhere else.

But how easy is it to get a new council flat? I'd be on a waiting list, and by the time they'd prioritised all the families also waiting, Evie would be long gone, and the demon inside would have taken her place on Earth.

I reach my arm back and punch the wall. It leaves a dent, and pieces crumble onto the tufts of carpet. Grace probably heard it too. So did Evie. The thing inside of her would laugh at me again.

I move away from the wall. Charge to the kitchen. I wish I hadn't left the wine next door. Doesn't matter, there's whiskey in the cupboard. I take a tumbler glass and pour out the last few drops of a dusty bottle and drink it straight.

I have to call April.

I know I do.

I can't let a girl suffer because I want to be left alone.

I bow my head. Lean against the chair, straightening my arms. I'm shaking. My God, I'm really shaking. Why am I shaking?

I hate that this is happening. I hate that my conscience compels me to stop being such a coward. I hate that I had to care enough to go next door and find out what was happening.

What would I even say to April?

Screw it.

I stand. Pick up the phone. Unlock it. Scroll to April's number.

My thumb hovers over it. All I need to do is press it and it will ring and we will speak. Or maybe she won't pick up. Oh please, don't pick up.

Without allowing myself to overthink it anymore, I press her name and the phone rings. I put it to my ear and feel my stomach churn.

It rings. Just as I hope she won't pick up, she does.

"Hello?"

I open my mouth.

Just air comes out.

I stutter over syllables that don't arrive.

I try to form the words, but I can't.

"Hello?"

Hi.

Hey.

How are you?

I need your help.

Someone else needs your help.

I need... you.

I bow my head. Close my eyes. Run my hand through my hair.

"Mo, is that you?"

I grow alert. My body stiffens.

Dammit, my name would have come up when I called. How could I be so stupid?

"Mo, please just talk to me."

Should I talk? Should I hang up? What should I do?

"Mo, you've obviously called me for a reason, and I'm here, ready to listen, so please—"

I hang up.

I stare at my phone, as if it's going to explode.

A few seconds go by, and the screen lights up, and it's April, and she's calling me back.

I don't answer.

And when it finishes ringing, I wait for an answerphone message, but one doesn't arrive. And she doesn't call again.

I turn the phone off and put it in the kitchen drawer.

I don't know why I'm hiding it, treating it like an alien object that doesn't belong here, but somehow I fear it, and I don't want it anywhere near me.

I open my cupboard and search behind old boxes of cereal and stale bread. I find another almost-finished bottle of something. Gin, I think. I pour it into the glass and take it into the living room.

I put the television on. It's late. I scroll through channels, but nothing's on—or, should I say, nothing good enough to disrupt my thoughts.

It doesn't take long until *it* starts again.

The walls vibrate, reminding me what lies next door. I hear the screaming and the pounding and, though I don't hear them, I sense Grace's tears, and I can't help but think about how much pain she's in.

I turn the volume up on the television.

A late-night chat show shouts over the noise, but doesn't drown it out. I change the channels. Eventually I get to *Babestation*, one of the dodgy channels with the naked women on the phone. The brunette on the screen has lips too big and obviously fake breasts. I've never seen someone less attractive, yet the caption at the bottom promises the ability to listen in on her conversation for £1.50 a minute. I can't imagine what she'd possibly have to say that would be worth paying that much to listen to.

Then again, maybe some company would be nice.

I laugh. I can't help it. Am I really at the point I'm considering phoning hideous late-night porn stars just for someone to chat to? I wouldn't even care about the things she'd say she'd do to me; it would be nice just to make small talk about the weather.

I scoff. Chuckle into my gin.

What is the point of me?

No, really—what is the point?

I am insignificant. Unwanted. Lonely.

No one would notice if I left this world. God could squash me like a bug, and people would step over me to avoid the mess.

I keep watching the woman on the screen. Eventually, she changes to a new woman. A blond. She wears too much lip gloss, and her buttocks ripple as she shakes them.

The next thing I know, my eyes are opening, the sun is glaring at me through the window, and the television screen displays a sign saying the channel is now off air.

Good. Those women deserve a break.

We all do.

Evie Speaks

I don't know where I go or how I get there.

Sometimes I just open my eyes, and I am there. My feet might be bare and covered in soil, or they might be in bright white socks covered in sap, or they might be like the other day when I was wearing a pair of shoes I didn't recognise, with my calves smeared in dog faeces.

I'm often wearing my nightie, or Mummy's clothes; one time, I woke up in the woods and I was wearing nothing but plain white underwear. I rushed back, desperate not to be seen. One man passed me and stopped, but I ran faster so he couldn't say anything, and he disappeared from view.

Today, I am wearing a dark red dress with frills around the base and straps over my shoulders. It stops halfway down my thigh, revealing my legs in a way that the nuns at our old church would say causes boys to have impure thoughts. I'm not wearing a bra and fabric ends in the shape of a V over my cleavage. I hold my arms over my chest to cover myself and shiver from the cold.

I am taller because I'm wearing high heels—I've never worn high heels before, and they aren't very comfortable. The labels are still attached to the dress. I feel them pricking my neck. I pull them off. They say the dress is £210, marked down from £260. I don't recognise the name of the shop they've come from. And I don't know how I got this dress. Just like I don't know what time it is.

But I know where I am.

I am outside the gates of my school. The sky is grey, and the school looks dim, but there are still students inside the classrooms—I can see their heads through the windows—so it must be during school hours. I grip the fence like it's bars from a prison cell and peer inside.

Funnily enough, I don't miss this place. I just miss having somewhere to go.

"I thought I told you to leave."

A voice, stern and womanly, comes from my right. A teacher is walking toward me. I think her name is Mrs Matilda. She is one of the deputy heads, and she is very strict and never smiles. Keys jangle as she walks. She wears a suit jacket over a white blouse and smart trousers, and she holds a walkie talkie.

She thinks she needs to dress like a man to be in authority.

We laugh at the stupidity of this teacher. Somehow, I know she's going through a divorce from her second husband and that they hate each other. They never had children, even though her husband wanted them. They could never conceive, and it has made her feel like less of a woman. She finds it tough to be around her friends, because they all have children, and she doesn't. She's approaching forty, and she doesn't have many years of fertility left.

"I told you to leave, didn't I? You are suspended, Evie."

"Why don't you have children?"

I don't know why we say it. I don't move my lips, but I hear my voice saying the words and I have no control over them being said.

"Excuse me?"

"I said, how come you don't have kids?"

"Evie, I'm not quite sure what you are playing at–"

"Was it him, or was it you?"

"Excuse me?"

I see it. In her face. It lasts a second, then she hides it again, but I know it was there. She broke, just for a moment.

"Is that why you're divorcing him? So you don't have to look at the man who you couldn't give a child?"

She stops walking toward me. Stares at me. The look on her face is priceless. We enjoy it very much. She doesn't know what to say.

"How do you know this, Evie?"

I just grin.

"Have you been spying on me? Listening in on my phone conversations?"

"No one cares about you enough to spy on you. Even your soon-to-be-ex-husband won't return your calls. He's too busy having the time of his life without you."

She points a long, spindly finger at me. "You need to leave. I have already called your mother and told her what you've done."

What I've done?

"We need to discuss this with the governors, but I can't see a likely return for you if this is what you are willing to do to get back at us."

"What I am willing to do?"

"Yes, Evie, what you are willing to do."

"I don't know what you mean."

She narrows her eyes and shakes her head. "Really, Evie, please don't bother. We are showing your mother the CCTV right now."

"What?"

Mummy is here? When did Mummy get here? How did she get here?

"I don't understand."

"Right, well, maybe the police will be better at getting through to you."

The police?

I try to think. Try to remember. What did I do? Where was I?

The school sign.

I did something to the school sign.

I rush past Mrs Matilda, ignoring her cry for me to stop, and I reach the main gate and I look at the sign. The name of the school is unintelligible, just as is the slogan beneath it, as it is smeared in human faeces.

I look down at my hands.

They are mostly clean, but there are scrapes of dark and light brown on some of my fingers. Small chunks in my finger-nails. I'm not wearing underwear and my buttocks feel uncomfortably filthy.

"No... I didn't do this..."

She's laughing. Inside of me. *She* finds this hilarious. And *she* suddenly allows me to remember. The dress is on the floor. My hands are below my crotch. Catching it. Spreading it and smearing it. Until every inch is covered. But it's not on my hands anymore, so...

Oh my God.

My tongue.

I taste it.

I licked myself clean. Like an animal.

I did this.

Oh, God, I did this.

Then I took the dress from someone's locker, and I wore it and replaced it with...

Good girl, Evie. Good girl.

I fall to my knees. I cry. I feel my stomach, and I feel sick, and it lurches to my throat, but I have eaten nothing so all that I spew is blood and bile.

Mummy walks out of the building. There are police officers

with her. Two of them. Men. Big and strong. They are going to hurt us, I know they are, so I turn, and I run.

I hear Mrs Matilda shout for me, but I don't listen, I just run, and I keep running, the inside of my legs pulling at something that's crusted on my skin.

I pass the field where a dog chases me then gets bored, past the bakers where Mummy buys her bread, and past the lake where we once fed the ducks, until I arrive home, but they are already there, waiting for me.

Mummy and the police officers.

The police have a piece of paper. They say it's from the school, and that I have to show up at court. We know we won't go to court. *She* will never allow it.

And I hate this police officer. More than anything. At this moment, I feel nothing but rage at the sight of his face.

Then *she* takes over again, and I don't know what happens next.

But I'm sure I will when I wake up, and we are together again.

THIRTEEN

I pick up the phone.

I need a woman. Desperately. The kind of caress only a female hand can give. The kind that electrifies you— the kind that reminds you that you exist.

The kind you have to pay for.

She's caring—but only because I pay her to be. The movies teach you that people are mostly good, and that bad people lose. They could not be more wrong. From what I've witnessed, whenever a person has a choice to be nasty or nice, ninety percent of the time they choose nasty—unless they are being paid.

"I'll be round in fifteen," Ramona says, and I put the phone down and wonder how I'm going to pay for it.

I open the internet banking app on my phone. An offer for a credit card comes up straight away. I hit the apply button, and within minutes I have a £2500 credit limit to use. I don't know why anyone would give that to me, but I have it, and it will be enough.

I perch on the windowsill. Drum my fingers against the

glass, leaving smudges in the condensation. A woman walks past with a pram in one hand, dragging a crying child in another, and a cigarette held between her lips. Her heavy footsteps grow quieter as she marches out of sight.

I look toward next door. I can't see the front of their home, but I can see their faded welcome mat. I bow my head. I feel bad. But I'm used to it. I spend most of my days feeling bad about something or other. Sometimes it's something I did years ago, a passing comment that I regretted and have ruminated about ever since. It usually passes after I manage to convince myself I don't care.

The familiar clops of high heels grow louder. By the time she reaches my flat, I am at the door, holding it open for her. She wears dark red lipstick and black mascara. Her boots are black and knee high, revealing a bit of thigh at the end of her black dress. She wears a coat, open over her busty cleavage.

"Hey," she says, and kisses me hard, like she means it, then pulls away and smiles. "How are you?"

Her voice is sweet and soft, like it could melt all over me. People are always so focussed on how a person looks or smells, they don't always realise how sexy someone's voice could be. Everything about her dulcet tone oozes sex. She is the reason the act was invented.

She puts her hands on my belt and unbuckles it. I'm excited by her, but I feel... I don't know. *Off.* Like this isn't what I want. Not right now, anyway.

I take her by the arms, and I tell her, "Stop."

"What's the matter?" she says, smiling, cupping me, feeling me grow hard as she looks up at me and raises her eyebrows.

"It's just... Can we wait?"

"Wait? I charge by the hour, you know."

She winks at me. I like it.

"I mean, I just—I'm not feeling great this evening."

"Then why did you call me?"

It's a good question. Why did I call her?

Have I really gotten to the point I'm going to pay a prostitute simply for the company?

"How about we go out to dinner?" I say.

"Dinner? Don't you want to fuck?"

"Yes. No. Maybe later. I don't know. I just... I feel like I want to talk. Get to know you."

"You don't want to get to know me. You want to see me naked."

She smiles again and giggles playfully, making her hand even firmer around my dick.

"I'm not messing around," I tell her. "I want to take you to dinner."

She stops cupping me. Steps back. Narrows her eyebrows and looks at me peculiarly.

"You're serious, aren't you?"

"Yeah. I just want to go out. Eat. Talk. I don't know, it sounds nice."

"You do know you will have to pay me by the hour? It could get costly."

I think of the £2500 credit limit on the card. "I can afford it."

"If you're sure? I mean, you're paying for the time, so..."

"Yeah, I am. Let me grab my coat."

She raises her hands into the air to display her reluctant acceptance, and I walk to the cupboard and open it, ignoring the smell of damp. I take my brown jacket and put it on. Then pause.

What am I doing?

No. Let's not second guess it. Let's just do what I want.

It's been a long time since I bought a woman dinner.

I call a taxi and he takes us into town. We find a nice,

quaint tapas place down a lit alleyway with outside seating under heaters. Ramona says she'd rather avoid the smokers, so we go inside, and we sit at the window. I take off her jacket and she thanks me. A few men look at her revealing dress, but a scowl from me makes them look away. When a waitress comes over, I decide on which tapas items we want. This is my time, after all.

After the waitress brings us some plates and our drinks—a beer for me and a white wine for her—we take a sip, then we look at each other, and an awkward silence unlike I've ever had with her begins.

Then again, I suppose we've never left much room for silence before. There's always the blissful quiet that comes after sex, but that's not uncomfortable. This is.

But she looks at me, smiling, expecting me to say something.

"So," I say. "Where do you come from?"

"Around."

"Where did you grow up?"

"A place."

"What hobbies do you enjoy?"

"Stuff."

I frown. "Why are you being so elusive?"

She chuckles. "Because you don't really want to know the answers to these questions."

"Yes, I do."

"But you don't pay me to know the boring stuff about my life. You pay me to be your fantasy."

"Right now, I'm paying you to be my date."

"Then let me be the date you want me to be."

"You would be, if you answered the questions."

She smiles. Looks down at her drink. Nods, as if giving herself permission to answer the questions.

"Fine," she says. "I grew up in London—Kensington, the

posh part. I went to boarding school. My parents were politicians. Well, my dad was—my mum gave it up when she had me. They retired last year and have gone to live in Spain."

"You can't be serious."

"Why not?"

"You're lying. You're just pretending."

"Why? A posh girl can't become an escort?"

"You have a million choices for what you want to be. You come from privilege. I mean, your parents love each other, what happened?"

"What do you mean, what happened?"

"Well, why did you end up..."

"As a whore? Is that what you're trying to say?"

I shrug. "Fine."

"You are so judgemental." She leans back and folds her arms.

"How am I judgemental?"

"You think a woman can't just choose this life? Can't decide to be empowered by taking advantage of her looks? Can't just enjoy sex and want to earn money doing what she loves?"

"Well, honestly, no."

"No?"

"I don't get why you'd go into your line of work without some kind of, I don't know, fucked up childhood."

"I'm not some street whore, Mo. I don't take crack and hang around on the corner. I am a professional, and I cater for-"

"Fine, fine." I wave my hand around. "I didn't mean to offend you."

She raises her eyebrows. "Oh, I'm not offended."

"You sure?"

"Unless you want me to be."

"Why would I want you to be?"

"I don't know. You're paying for this, remember? I can be whatever you want."

"How about you just be yourself?"

Our first plate of tapas arrives. It's pork meatballs in a BBQ sauce. The next two arrive with another waitress. Sweet potato and beef stew, and pulled pork.

We eat. I place dollops onto my plate, not realising how hungry I am, whilst Ramona places a few bits on her plate and pokes at it.

The next few plates arrive shortly after, and we don't talk until they are almost finished.

"So who is it you love?" she asks, breaking the silence.

"What?"

"You are telling me about the stereotypes of escorts—well I'll tell you about the stereotypes of clients. They are normally heartbroken. Fixated on an ex. The one that got away. Sometimes they stalk her. A few even ask me to wear a wig and dress like her."

"Those guys sound fucked up."

"We're all fucked up."

"Ain't that the truth?"

I finish a mouthful and take a few sips of beer.

"So who is she? This ex you cling onto?"

"Ah, see, that's where your assessment is wrong. She's not an ex."

"But there is someone."

I shrug. "You said there is, so I guess so."

"So why is she not an ex?"

"She is in love with someone else."

"And she won't leave him?"

"More that she won't forget him."

"I see. And what, you decided not to wait for her?"

I lean back in my chair. Most of the tables are now empty. It must be getting late. When did that happen?

"Why don't you just move on from her?"

I shake my head. "It's not that simple."

"It is. It's just a decision you make—that you're over her."

"That easy, is it?"

"Focus on what is bad about her."

"What if there's nothing bad about her?"

"There's always something bad. Maybe she chews with her mouth open, or she's high maintenance, or she's stupid for not being over this other guy."

"Stupid? You're saying she's stupid?" My leg bounces. I feel agitated. My heart quickens pace. I feel an anger rise in me that I'm not sure I can control.

"Only stupid in the sense that–"

"You know what? Fuck you. You know nothing."

"I'm just saying–"

"Then don't. She is ten times the woman you are. No, scrap that—*a hundred* times. Compared to her, you are a dung beetle. The stupidest of the stupids. She is a goddess, and you are just a diseased little slut."

For the first time, I see her break. Her eyes narrow. Her playful expression is gone. I've just ruined something within her. I can see that. And she refuses to let herself cry in front of a client.

"To hell with this," she says, and she gets up, and she charges toward the door.

I watch her go. And I sigh. And I realise what I've done, and when will I ever learn? No one ever says or does anything useful when the red mist arrives.

With a huff, I push myself up from my seat and run outside, and I see her marching toward the taxi rank, drying her eyes.

I run up to her, grab her arm and turn her around, and she pulls her arm away from me.

"Don't touch me," she says, and that body I find so inviting suddenly seems so far away.

"Listen, I... I'm sorry. I..."

She folds her arms and raises her eyebrows.

"I thought you were being paid to be who I wanted you to be, anyway?" I say.

Immediately, I know it was the wrong thing to say.

She turns to go, then stops as I shout, "Hey, wait!"

She looks at me expectantly, and, without knowing what else to say, I blurt out, "I haven't paid you yet."

She glares at me. I take out my phone.

"Can I transfer it to you?"

She folds her arms. "It's fine."

"What? No, come on. I said I would."

"You bought dinner. Let's just call it even."

"No, really, I–"

She steps toward me and puts a hand on my chin. The softness of her skin soothes me.

"It's fine," she says, and I put my phone away. "Because I feel sorry for you. That's right, Mo—me, a diseased little slut, feels sorry for *you*."

She holds her hand out and a taxi stops. I watch her get in and leave. Then I return to the restaurant and pay, collect my jacket, and trudge home.

It's an hour's walk, and it's raining, but I don't care. I deserve the ache in my legs and the soaking of my skin. I cross the street slowly, passing couples with their arms around each other and teenagers hanging around on the street with nothing better to do.

When I finally arrive home, hobbling up the stairs whilst brushing rainwater out of my eyes, I go to open my door, and pause.

There is scuffling.

Coming from inside.

I place my ear against the door.

I hear it. Movement. Like someone, or something, is scratching at the walls.

And I open the door, knowing I am not alone.

EVIE SPEAKS

Somehow, I know I'm in a police station.

That much is clear.

I don't know how I know, but I know. Even though I'm in a toilet cubicle. My dress is around my ankles. The walls smell like fresh paint. I look in the bowl and I see blood. It's also on my leg. Bright red. I have no pad, but I hope that there will be a machine in the bathroom.

I flush the toilet. Stand. Put my dress back on. Then I hear voices.

Male voices.

I look back at the toilet seat I was sitting on. Specks of urine decorate it.

Is this bathroom unisex?

I crouch on the floor, placing my hands on the solid, cold ground, not caring for the filth I am kneeling in. I feel so disgusting that I'm not sure it will make much difference.

I peer out from beneath the space below the door. I see the back of two men's ankles. They are standing at urinals. You wouldn't have a urinal in a unisex bathroom. Which means I'm in the *men's* bathroom.

Why am I here?

I watch the men's ankles. They talk about menial things, like sports and time off and bad weather. Eventually, they shake and zip up. One of them washes his hands. The other doesn't. Then they both walk out.

Taking my opportunity, I rush out of the cubicle, almost tripping over my own feet. I catch sight of myself in the mirror. Mascara smudges in my eyes. I've never worn mascara before. The people at my church said it was impure to decorate myself like a hussy. I don't even know how to apply it. So how do I have it on?

And am I wearing lipstick as well?

I turn to the door, but it creaks open before I can leave. A man walks in. Dressed as a police officer, though he looks like a child. He is young, maybe early twenties. Innocent eyes, dimples on his cheeks.

He doesn't look shocked to see me.

In fact, he looks quite excited to see me.

He locks the door to the men's bathroom, then turns to the cubicles. He kicks each door open, ensuring there is no one in there, then he stands, feet shoulder width apart, panting, arms by his sides, body hunched over. There is something in his eyes that scares me, but I'm not sure why.

"Well, I'm here," he says. His voice is husky and creepy. I don't like it.

I look over my shoulder, sure that he couldn't be talking to me. But we're alone and locked in. Of course he's talking to me.

"Oh, don't play hard to get now. You told me to meet you in here when the coast is clear." He steps toward me. "Well, the coast is clear."

I want Mummy. This man is strange. His stare is like a dog's when someone tries to take away its food. It's carnal and aggressive. Protective in a way that does not make me feel protected.

"I don't know what—"

Shush, my love.

What is he doing?

What we asked him to.

I don't understand.

Just follow my lead.

I step toward him. Look up at his face. He's so much taller than me. Our reflection is in my periphery, and I don't recognise myself in it. My face is grey and intense. There's something animalistic about the way my body stands.

"Take off your pants," we tell him.

"Hey, don't you want to—"

"I said take off your pants."

He doesn't argue. He hurriedly removes his duty belt and places it on the sink. He undoes his trouser belt and lets his trousers drop to his feet, along with his white briefs.

His cock leans to the left. It's small, kind of like a slug.

"Are you not hard for us?"

He both smiles and frowns at the same time. "I thought that you might—"

We grab it. He jumps.

"Your hands are cold."

We smile. He smiles. Then he grows confused.

"Are you not going to rub it?" he says. "You kind of need to—"

We squeeze a little.

"Ah, okay! Not what I was thinking, but—"

We squeeze harder.

"No, stop it, I—"

We squeeze even harder, and he recoils, bending over. His hands move loosely toward us, but he doesn't grab us or touch us in fear of what we might do.

"Stop it, I don't like—"

We squeeze and pull.

"Oh my God, what are you doing?"

We squeeze harder. We feel it press against our fingers. We pull, expecting it to come off like a pen lid, but it doesn't.

"Fuck! Stop!"

It feels mushy. Like those peas Mummy makes us eat. All gross and nasty.

He puts a hand on our neck, tries to squeeze, tries to threaten us. We grab his arm with our spare hand and bite his wrist. Blood dribbles between our teeth and he stops grabbing us.

"Fucking stop it, you're hurting me, this ain't fucking funny, this—argh!"

We squeeze harder and pull harder and squeeze and pull and squeeze and pull and he cries, whimpers, like a wailing child, and this is when *she* tells me to close my eyes, this is when *she* tells me to relax and let *her* take the stress away.

I sink back, like falling onto a comfy sofa, and I feel *her* arms around me and *she* loves me and I feel so good.

When I open my eyes, I'm outside, and I'm running. Fast. Sprinting. There's blood on my hands and I don't know where it came from. There's a bit of flesh stuck between my nails.

I am panting, and I stop, lean against a small, thin tree, and wait for my breathing to calm down.

I thought I was being chased, but there's no one behind me. I stare into the distance, looking in all directions, but there is no one. I'm on a green in the middle of an estate, and it's dark except for a lamppost and a few lights in bedrooms.

I feel suddenly hungry. Painfully so, like my belly is too empty.

I turn and run and, though I don't know the way, but *she* does, and *she* guides me.

Ten minutes later, we're back on our home estate. A group of men hang around on a bench. Tracksuits and shaved heads.

"All right, beautiful?" one of them says.

"What are you doing tonight?" another asks.

We turn and we look at them.

They step back. I don't know what it is, but they see something in our face that they don't like, and suddenly I'm not such a pretty girl to pick on anymore.

I run up the stairs and across the outside corridor. We are too hungry for whatever nonsense Mummy has. But the man's flat is next door. The man whose daddy killed himself. The man who thinks he knows who we are.

I feel a wrath glowering inside of me, and it spreads through my body like wildfire, and we turn, and we leap, and next thing I know, we're in a dark kitchen.

This isn't our flat.

But there are scraps of food.

And we help ourselves to it.

And we wait for him to come home.

FOURTEEN

I step into my home. It's colder than it was before. A faint shuffling cuts through the silence. Flickers of movement in the darkness come from the kitchen.

I close the door behind me.

"Hello?"

I edge forward. It could be a rat. It could be a burglar.

Or it could be something else entirely.

"Who's there?"

I turn the hallway light on. An overbearing amber glow illuminates the cracks in the hallway. I almost trip over a pair of stray shoes. I look down and find more items of mine on the floor—television remote, books, clothes.

I hear munching. Sloppy, open-mouthed munching.

I step over the items strewn over the worn-out carpet and enter the kitchen. The hallway light reveals a dark figure in the corner, crouched over.

"Evie?"

I turn the kitchen light on. She screams and I quickly turn it off again.

"Evie, is that you?"

She has the body of a sixteen-year-old girl, but the manner-isms of a decrepit, senile old man. Each movement is jilted. Each bone moves in a way it shouldn't. She looks feral.

"Evie, are you okay?"

My automatic reaction is to ask what she's doing here. But Evie didn't come here.

The thing inside of her did.

I get closer, and the light from the hallway reveals a little more about her appearance. She is wearing a revealing red dress—one that I am sure her mother would not approve of. Bright red blood is crusted down her leg. Her arms are muddy. There's shit in her fingernails.

"Why don't you turn around so I can talk to you?"

Her face turns to the side. Greasy strands of hair hang over her greying face. It's not even pale anymore—it's faded. Marks decorate her cheeks. Her lips are cracked and bleeding. Her body is hunched over. She holds a box of expired cereal, shov-elling handfuls of crunchy bits into her mouth. Most of it falls on the floor.

"Evie, what are you–"

I stop. Decide to change tact.

"It's not Evie I'm talking to right now, is it?"

It grins. Keeps shovelling the cereal between her cracked lips. Laughs a slow, croaky laugh.

"Why don't you tell me what your name is, so I know who I'm dealing with?"

"*My name – my name – my name – my name...*"

Her voice comes out in whispers, but it does not come from her. The words hit me from all sides, like surround sound, like she is all around me.

"You think you can trick me? Scare me? Please. I've seen plenty of your friends, and none of them scared me."

Its croaky laugh becomes longer, stretched out, *haaaaaaah, haaaaaaah, haaaaaaah.*

"I've faced plenty of you before. You won't–"

"*What about—the one—the girl—you lost—she killed—her family died—all dead—so you left—you lost then—did you not—you lost then...*"

It's right.

But I don't admit that.

This is what demons do.

It knows its enemy.

It knows my past, and it uses it against me. I mustn't let it win. I was foolish the other day, and I mustn't be foolish now.

"It's time to go home," I say. "Come on."

I step forward and reach out to touch her, to guide her home, but it flinches, then quickly turns and grabs my wrist.

Its grip is hard and tight. I try to turn my wrist out of its grip, but it's too strong, and it holds on and grins at me as it watches me squirm, then tightens its hold even harder, until I get pins and needles in my hands.

"Let go."

It watches me. Pupils fully dilated. Cracked lips spread from cheek to cheek in morbid delight.

This is not the strength of a sixteen-year-old girl.

"I said let go."

It grips even harder still, and paraesthesia sets in on my fingers as my hand goes numb.

It rises to her feet, steps toward me, stray pieces of cereal crunching beneath the soles of her feet. I back up, but this only encourages it. I reach the sink and can't back up any further and its body is against mine and I can feel the rancid aroma of her rotting breath stroking my chin.

It reaches its hand toward my crotch and I block it.

"That's enough."

"*Oh, come on—Mr Exorcist—you are better than that—better than that—why don't you stop me—stop me—oh stop me, please.*"

I consider taking a knife from the kitchen drawer, but that would hurt Evie, not this thing. So I raise my spare hand and bring my fist it down upon her arm with all the force of my body and she falls to her knees, and suddenly she's crying.

She looks up at me. Those are a girl's eyes. Her body doesn't hunch anymore. The demon has stepped back so Evie could feel the pain of my strike.

She holds her arm and looks around.

"Where am I?" she asks between sobs.

I stand her up. Put a hand on her back. Check her arm, but it's only bruised, she will be okay.

"You're in my flat. I live next door to you. How about I take you back to your home, yeah?"

She looks around, confused. It's amazing how her face can transform from malevolence to vulnerability so quickly. There is no more grinning, just fear. No more cackles, just tears in the corners of her eyes.

"This way, come on."

With an arm around her, I help her hobble through the hallway until we reach the door, and I steady her as we step outside.

I make brief eye contact with the lads on the green. They all turn and look at me, falling silent, glaring as I walk with my arm around a teenage girl, and I know they are misinterpreting the situation.

But I don't care.

It's none of their business.

Still, I feel their stares, and I wish they would turn away.

I knock on Grace's door. She answers it, a phone by her ear, then quickly hangs up and throws her arms around her daughter.

"Oh, Evie, I've been so worried!" she says, then turns to me. "Where was she?"

"I found her in my kitchen."

"Oh, Evie! How on earth did you end up there?"

She doesn't answer. Grace guides her in, then turns to me and says, "Thank you."

"Wait," I say, and block the door as she goes to close it.

Grace doesn't turn to me fully.

"Grace, let me see your eye."

"It's nothing."

"Grace, please."

She turns and looks at me. There is a faint black bruise around the eye she was trying to conceal.

"How did you get that?"

"Oh, you know."

"No, I don't know, Grace. How did you—"

"It really doesn't matter."

I shake my head. "Evie did it, didn't she?"

"Evie is a good girl."

"Grace?"

"... Fine. Yes. But it's okay. She's sick. She doesn't know what she's doing."

"Grace—"

"Thank you for your help," she says, and she closes the door before I can respond.

I stand there, considering knocking again, or just going in and talking to her.

But what would I say?

What can anyone say?

I turn away with my head down. Put my hands in my pockets. Walk slowly back to my door.

And I notice the group of lads. Still staring at me. Still wondering what I'm doing.

I ignore them, step inside my flat, and lock the door.

FIFTEEN

It starts again late at night.

It's part of the routine now.

The screaming. The shaking walls. The battering, inches away from my head, on the other side of a flimsy barrier.

I have now removed everything from the bookshelf, so only puffs of dust can fall to the floor. I've moved the bed away from the wall, though the bedroom is too small for me to move it too far and it didn't make much difference. I've also tried stuffing cotton wool in my ears, only to take them out ten minutes later—they do nothing to quell the noise.

The girl needs an exorcism.

But am I the right person to do it?

I'm not supposed to. They warned me about unsanctioned exorcisms the first time I met the Sensitives—a message given to me by April's stern voice. I'd just been fired from a job on a building site at the time, and I was standing in a queue at the job centre when my phone started ringing. It was a number I didn't know. I answered it anyway. I was told there was a job for me. Something that would be worthwhile. I asked who it was, and they said it would be explained.

I questioned it, but not enough to put off my curiosity. After all, I didn't care about my life, and I didn't know what I had to lose.

When I arrived, they led me into a small room with five other people, each looking as confused as I felt. They were all younger than me, fresh-faced and eager, and I wondered if I'd ever looked like that.

April told us who we were. I was drawn to her even then. Her punky fashion sense, her purple hair, her cheeky smile. I was already in love.

Unfortunately, I was yet to learn that the cheeky smile that intrigued me so much belonged to someone else.

She explained what a Sensitive is. That Heaven conceived us to be warriors in the ongoing battle against Hell. That demons existed, and they attacked people, infesting their homes and tormenting their bodies. That we were born with an inherent gift that made us sensitive to detecting and fighting supernatural attacks. She said that it is a gift, and that we should treat it as such.

Now, when one is told such a truth, one is right to be sceptical. I was an agnostic, and I believed in thinking things through, and looking at the evidence—I'd caused too much pain in my time by acting impulsively. But I didn't question it. Not even one bit. Because, for the first time in my life, I was being told something that actually made sense.

All my life, I had seen things. Sometimes out of the corner of my eye, sometimes stood blatantly in front of me. Glimpses of faces, or figures, or creatures with multiple heads or bodies of animals. I'd see their form in the mist, or in the shadows— but most of the time I'd see them in someone I walked past. I would look into their eyes, and a feeling would rise in my chest, a nauseous curiosity, and I would know something was wrong with them.

But I also knew that I couldn't know that.

It's strange, isn't it? How what you *know* for sure can change so drastically when someone offers a piece of information that fits perfectly.

They allocated us to more experienced Sensitives who would help us learn how to use our gifts. I was told to work with a man in his forties with light grey hair. I forget his name. He was quite standoffish, and he struggled to make eye contact. I assisted on multiple exorcisms, but I was always thinking about April, and when I would get to work with her.

Then I met a girl on the street. She was limping. Her skin looked tight around her bones. She wasn't right. I knew right then that I had to help her.

So I spoke to her parents and performed an exorcism. It was the first one I did on my own. I was cocky and thought it would impress April that I had done it.

It turned out she was not possessed, but that she was dying. She was ill and her parents were religious, and desperate to cling onto any hope that could be given to them. When the exorcism failed, I left the girl in a state of desperate pain. It devastated the parents that I could not fulfil my promises.

It's the only time I've ever heard April shout.

She told me we don't just go giving everyone we meet exorcisms. That it's rare that an exorcism is the solution to the person's problems, and ninety-nine times out of a hundred, the person needs psychological or medical help, and an exorcism will only exacerbate the situation.

She emphasised that we *never* perform an exorcism without the permission of the lead Sensitives. There was a hierarchy among us, and I was at the bottom, being told to listen to those at the top.

I wasn't hurt so much by her words, but by the way she

looked at me. Like I was an idiot. Like she regretted recruiting me.

I loved April from the first minute I saw her, but I could also see what was behind the veil of leadership. She gave everyone what they needed to grow and improve. She taught Sensitives how to harness their gifts and was always approachable when there was a problem. But, behind it, I could see pain. Loss. She missed the man she loved.

It was a pain I could never penetrate. She could not give her soul to someone else.

And now I lay on a broken mattress in a cheap council flat with crumbling walls and broken furniture, listening to the screams of a girl in pain, knowing that I must go against April's vehement instructions if I am to intervene.

But I also know that April wouldn't want a girl to be in pain.

Maybe Evie is just ill. But I've seen enough to convince myself otherwise. I just need to be sure.

And it is at this moment that I decide.

I will help her.

I will try to rid her of the demon once I have hard proof that it is there.

And I will try to restore love and hope to that broken home.

And I feel suddenly scared. Hopeless. Alone.

I've never fought a demon on my own before. It requires a group to fight it. Exorcisms can last hours, days, even weeks, and more than one person being present allows others to rest without the process stopping.

But I can't just let this girl suffer.

Though I know if I fail, it will just make things worse. The demon will surface and will become stronger.

And April would be even more disappointed in me should she find out.

I run my hands over my face. I can't live my life according to what April would want. I can't lay here every night replaying old memories like a tired home movie. I can't keep myself from doing the right thing because no one's here to tell me whether I should.

But, most of all, I can't keep myself from being scared.

Not for me, but for the poor, suffering girl.

For someone whose saviour is a pathetic, silly man like me.

Evie Speaks

I wake up like this every day. Head pounding. Neck sweaty. Whatever pyjamas or nightie I have on clings to my perspiration. My throat burns. My body aches—like I've been up all night, running or jumping or fighting.

I have a routine now.

First, I lay my head back on my pillow and rest. I feel more tired than when I went to bed. There is no light to wake me from the blacked-out windows, but the alarm clock tells me it's gone eleven in the morning.

Mummy doesn't even bother waking me up anymore.

She's scared of me.

She's scared of us.

Second, I try to remember any dreams. They are rarely coherent. They are usually just images or feelings. Like my stomach digesting, or my hands rummaging through dirt, or something inside of me, like a man or an object.

I've never so much as kissed a boy. God wishes me to show self-control and obedience, and I do this through self-restraint. The Gospel of Peter says, "Beloved, I urge you as sojourners and exiles to abstain from the passions of the flesh, which wage war against your soul." So I do as I'm told. But I have these flickers of memory that feel so real—of a man's heaving breath, or his face sweating over mine, or feeling of something inside of me; something uncomfortable pressing against my cervix.

I will these thoughts away, as I do any thought that tempts me to passions of the flesh.

Finally, I sit up. I close my eyes so I can't see what I've done. Not yet. Then I take a deep breath, and I look down, wondering what I'm going to find on my body this morning.

Today, I open my eyes and look down at a sheet that used to be white. It's now grey with brown and green stains. Mummy won't change them because *she* won't let her, which means I have to sleep on sheets crusted with my excrement.

And it's covered in bloody handprints.

I turn my hands over. They are covered in blood. I lift my nightie. I can't find any wounds, so the blood can't be mine.

There's also something in my teeth. Between the incisors. I wipe my hand on the duvet and reach inside. I pull out a bit of raw meat attached to a few strands of fur. Then I cough and retch, and something lurches up my throat, and I vomit blood and bile. It's full of lumps, all of which look like pieces of meat. Except one bit, which is long and lightly coloured. It looks like a tail.

I stand. Back away from the bed.

What did I do?

The heel of my foot presses on something soft. It squelches. I feel it ooze beneath my skin.

I look down.

And I scream.

I'm standing on a rat.

A dead rat.

Its eyes are missing. Its belly is open. Its tail is gone.

I back up, and something else squelches beneath my foot, and I back up again and slip on something else.

I look around the room.

My God…

They are everywhere.

All over the floor.

Rat after rat after rat after rat after rat.

Some missing heads. Some missing tails. Some missing fur, or ears, or insides, or legs.

I feel another lurch in my belly, so violent it forces me to my knees, and I land on more carcasses as my mouth opens and vomit fires through my throat and projects onto the floor, coating the rats in my stomach juices, sending the missing pieces back to their owners.

My stomach feels suddenly empty. Minutes ago, I felt full, and now I feel queasy. It doesn't stop me from throwing up again, except this one is harder, and it brings up something bigger, and I have to open my mouth and cry as something forces its way through my throat and lands on the pool I've already left.

It's a head.

I leap to my feet and scream and jump back onto the bed and scream again.

"Mummy! Mummy!"

Footsteps pound through the hallway. Mummy enters, still in her dressing gown, her hair wild and unkempt. She has a faint black eye. How did she get that?

"Mummy! Help!"

She comes in and halts. She looks around. Then looks at me. She looks horrified. It hurts that she's so distraught, but I don't remember doing it, I don't, really I don't, and I don't know what's wrong with me.

There's nothing wrong with you.

Stop it, I don't like you!

Yes, you do.

No, I don't!

You love me, Evie. Because you need me. We need each other.

I bow my head. Cry. I don't know what to say or do or how to act or how to stop this incessant voice that whispers constantly into my ears, all the time, over and over, telling me bad things and telling me it loves me and that we belong together.

I don't know how to make it stop.

Mummy stops gaping and gasping long enough to whisper, "What have you done?"

"I don't know, Mummy," I sob. "I don't know. I don't remember doing it."

She steps further in, her hands over her mouth, but stays near enough to the doorway that she can escape at any moment.

"Please, Mummy, I'm scared, I'm really scared, she won't stop talking to me and–"

You tell her about me, and I'll make you gut her and eat her.

I bow my head. Cry into my hands. I can't say anything. I can't explain anything. I don't know how I'd even try.

She has me trapped.

I feel loved, and I feel wanted—but I don't feel respected.

Stop this nonsense, you little eejit.

I shake my head.

We are family, and family love each other.

"I'll—look—it's fine, it's okay," Mummy says, though she still doesn't approach me, and I can tell she doesn't mean it. "I'll clean it up. It will be okay."

She steps out of the room and re-enters a few minutes later with a large bin bag and a pair of tongs. She pulls a face, leaves again, then returns another minute later with a scarf wrapped around her nose and mouth.

Cautiously, she edges in and starts picking up pieces of rat with the tongs, stretching her arm as far away from her body as she can, whilst still being able to reach the carcasses, and places them in the bin bag.

The smell is awful. It's rank. Disgusting. It makes me feel sick, but I have nothing left to throw up.

I stay on my bed, like the floor is made of fire, and watch her on my knees. I sob, but I do it silently so as not to upset Mummy more than I already have.

And she whispers into my ear.

I'm not going anywhere, you know.

Please, this isn't good.

We are one, Evie. You need to realise that.

But I don't like this.

This is how it will always be.

No!

The pain will continue until you accept me.

Why can't you just leave?

I'm never leaving, Evie. Never.

Please...

Mummy notices my vomit. She picks a rat from among the juices, but doesn't take the pieces of flesh I puked up. She stares at the mess, as if trying to figure out the best way to dispose of them.

Then she carries on with the last few rats.

There is only one way for you to be content.

What?

You aren't going to like it.

Please.

It is the only way you won't keep experiencing all this pain.

I'll do it. Anything.

Promise?

Yes. What must I do?

Go.

What?

You must go. Leave your conscious mind and let me take control.

But then I'll be gone forever…

But you won't have to witness it anymore.

But Mummy…

You won't be with her again. You'll be able to see her, but from the back of your mind.

I don't want to leave Mummy.

But the pain, my darling.

What about the pain?

The pain will be gone.

It will?

All of it. I promise.

I feel an arm around me, though I know there isn't one.

Mummy finishes picking up the last rat and looks at me like she's trying to figure out how to solve a puzzle.

"Why don't you go in the shower?" she asks.

"I don't want to."

Mummy nods timidly, stares at me, and leaves.

But I decide she's right.

I go to the shower.

We go to the shower.

And as I stand under the showerhead, letting its hot water scald me, its full force pounding against my face, I feel *her* arms around me, guiding my hands downwards, until I feel them between my legs.

"No…" I whisper. "The passions of the flesh… I mustn't…"

Trust me.

"But, the works of flesh are evident, the–"

I said to trust me. This will all be over soon.

Her grip on my arms is too strong. *She* forces *her* arms downwards, and *she* shoves them against *our* skin. Drags them down. Until they reach my genitalia.

She pushes my left hand to our cunt. Our wet, juicy cunt. And *she* pushes it inside until it's submerged in moisture.

She holds my right hand between my labia. Drags it upwards, until I find a bump, small put definite, and *she* rubs it.

My breath quivers.

It's a feeling I've never felt before.

A sensation I wasn't expecting.

And both hands are rubbing, and *she's* guiding them, letting the shower wash over my face as my hands dirty my body.

That's it...

We rub harder.

Both hands become more vigorous.

My body shakes. My legs grow weak. My breath quickens.

And I enjoy it.

I actually enjoy it.

Our finger goes further inside, and we feel the warmth, and our other finger turns in circles, then up and down, gentle then fast then gentle then fast.

Then it's just fast.

And our breath quickens, and the passion of the flesh overtakes us, and we are against the wall and we experience what I thought was too sinful to experience.

Then my hands fall free. I look at them. At what I've done. At the perversion I've given into.

She made me do it.

She used my hands, but it was *her*.

And I hadn't said *she* could.

You see what we can have if you give in...

I do see. I see it all now.

Do you not think it's best I take over?

What about me?

You'll still be here. I'll let you sit beside me, sometimes. Other times, you can watch from the back.

Will it hurt?

Sometimes.

Will it hurt less?

Absolutely.

I bow my head. The water soaks my hair. My fingers stink.

Fine. Okay.

I give in.

I surrender.

I sink back, falling slowly, relaxing, melting into oblivion.

Then, suddenly, I'm here, but I'm watching. I'm away from the action, behind a window, battering against the glass with no one able to hear me.

She turns the shower off.

She'd rather be filthy.

She steps out of the shower and looks at her new naked body in the mirror.

It's beautiful, and it's dirty.

And she's going to fucking ruin it.

Sixteen

I feel nervous.

I don't know why.

I've done this before. Many times. Never unaccompanied, but I'm not incompetent. I know how it works. I know everything I need to do.

So why do I dread it so much?

I stand at my window, my hands in my pockets, churning up the fabric of my trousers. I think about eating, but I can't eat. Instead, I wait, my arms occasionally shaking, watching for when Grace leaves the flat.

It takes a while, but eventually she steps outside, a large black bin bag in her hand, and locks the door behind her.

Has the situation come to the point where she has to lock her daughter in when she goes out?

I scoff at myself. Of course it has. I know what these things are capable of. I have no doubt that it's forced Evie to leave the flat by now, in order to commit acts of violence, of deviance, and of sexual perversion—and Grace will have no choice but to contain her.

The poor girl.

The poor woman.

I time the exit from my flat to when I hear Grace's steps approaching her door. I step outside, and as I lock my door, I feign noticing Grace.

She looks worse. She looked bedraggled before; now she looks ill. It's not just the pale face or the bags under her eyes—it's the expression she wears. There's no hope left in it. She's worn down and ready to give up.

"Grace," I say. "I was hoping to run into you."

She keeps her head down and, without looking at me, forces a small, reluctant smile—one that is so brief I almost don't notice it.

Her eyes do not meet mine.

She puts the key in her door and turns it.

"Grace?"

She pauses, staring at the floor, turning in my direction but not lifting her head.

"I wondered if I might have a word?"

"I... I'm busy."

Her voice is quieter than a whisper. It's a broken utterance.

"I know, but I need to talk to you. It's quite important. It's about your daughter."

"What did she do?"

"Nothing, it's not like that. I wonder if I might be able to help. Could I come in?"

She pauses. I can see her considering saying no. But she is too desperate. She faintly nods and lets me in.

I glance over my shoulder. The group of lads stands on the green, scowling at me. I ignore them and shut the door behind me.

It is pitch black. I go to turn a light on, but Grace quickly turns and snaps, "No!"

I take my hand away.

"The light, it—it's too much. I'll light some candles."

We enter the kitchen. It stinks of rotten eggs and expired milk. The pile of dishes in the sink has grown bigger since the last time I was here. A few flies hover around them.

I take a seat at the table and place my hands on my lap; I cannot find a clean part of the table for me to rest my elbows on.

Within a few minutes, Grace has lit a few candles, and I can see her face in the flickering amber glow.

She sits opposite me.

She says nothing.

"Are you okay?" I ask, then feel stupid for asking it.

Fortunately for me, she doesn't answer.

"You said you wanted to talk?" she eventually says.

"Yes, I do. I guess I should just say what I have to say—but, please, don't dismiss me straight away. I'm about to tell you the truth."

Grace sighs. She isn't interested. She focuses her gaze on the hallway, where the door to Evie's bedroom is. So I get on with it.

"I'm an exorcist," I blurt out.

Now she looks at me.

"I belonged to a group of people called the Sensitives," I continue. "We are paranormally gifted. I left because..." I decide not to tell her about people being murdered at an exorcism. "... Well, we fell out, and I left. That's why I came here, I guess."

She looks bemused. I don't blame her. I think most people would tell me where to go—but she doesn't. Whether that's because she's willing to entertain my claim, or just a lack of energy, I don't know.

"I believe your daughter is possessed, Grace. By a demon. And she is not just in the early signs of possession, either—she is in the latter stages, and if we don't act quickly, the demon will take Evie's body, and Evie will be lost forever."

Her eyes narrow into a glare.

"It might still be too late," I persist, before she can object. "It doesn't always work this late in a possession. But I still think it's worth a try. And I might be the only person you know that can help."

I stop talking. Let the words settle and hover between us like a dark cloud.

She doesn't speak at first. She just stares. Weary and fed up. I think back to how polite and lovely she was just a few weeks ago, and how keen she was to help her daughter.

This is a woman who's grieving for a child she hasn't even lost yet. I've seen it before. The eyes. How the person they are seems to fade away. A demon doesn't just torment its victim— it torments the victim's family, too.

"Grace?" I prompt her. "Grace, I need you to say something."

She looks around. Crosses her legs. Folds her arms.

"My Evie," she says slowly, spitting each word, "is not *possessed*. She has not got a *demon* inside of her. My girl is *sick*."

"Really, I–"

"Is this because I'm Catholic? You decide to make fun of us because you can see that we are devout, religious folk who don't give into temptations like everyone else? That we follow the Bible properly, unlike all these charlatans who go to church on Sunday after drinking and fornicating on Saturday night?"

"Grace, I'm not taking advantage."

"Then what are you doing? Trying to mess with me? This is my daughter, and when it comes to my daughter, I do not appreciate being messed with."

I lean toward her. "Grace, please, I–"

"I think you should leave. I think you should never disturb us again."

I lean back. Consider doing as she asks, envisioning myself figuring, hey, I gave it a go.

But I feel the evil emanating from the door across the hallway.

And that girl deserves my help.

"I can prove it to you," I say.

She scowls and turns away.

"I can. I can prove it enough to quell any disbelief. And I can do it now."

"You can't prove–"

"Fine, if I can't, then I will do as you ask. I will leave, and I will never bother you again. We'll just be neighbours who pass in the hall. But if there is even a part of you that wonders, even out of curiosity, whether this is true—then I ask you, please, give me half an hour in there, with Evie, and with you there, then I will present my proof."

She huffs. Takes her time to think about it. Uncrosses her legs and crosses them the other way.

"If you so much as hurt my daughter one bit, Mr Iscariot, I will have you arrested."

"And you would be right to do so."

She shakes her head. "I can't believe I'm agreeing to this."

"You are doing the right thing. I promise."

She looks at me and raises her eyebrows.

"Well?" she says.

I stand. "I will just collect some things, then we will begin."

And that is how I re-enter a war I thought I'd left.

I do not let Grace see I am afraid.

Or out of my depth.

Or incredibly stupid for battling a demon this imbedded in its host on my own.

I just collect my things and meet her in Evie's bedroom, ready for my next big mistake.

SEVENTEEN

I pause by the bedroom door with a bag of items in my hand. Grace stands over my shoulder.

I give the same warning I always do.

"When I provoke it, it may simulate pain, it may say or do nasty or obscene things, and it may pretend to be suffering—don't buy it. We are dealing with something that is not human; it is evil. You cannot reason with evil."

"You sound like a cliché, Mo."

I nod. "I do."

I place my hand on the door handle. Something fires up my arm. I can already feel what I'm dealing with. It has grown stronger, and is getting stronger by the hour. There may have been moments where Evie could regain control a few days ago, but those instances will have become infrequent, and soon there will be nothing left of her to save.

With a deep breath, I enter the room.

She sits on the bed. Cross-legged. Hands on her knees. Body still. She smiles a demented smile, and her eyes follow me through the room.

"Shut the door," I instruct Grace, then add, "please."

She does as I ask.

I place a few candles on the dresser behind me. I light them. I'd prefer the light on, but I do not want to distress it. Not yet. I want to gather my evidence before I harm it.

"Hello, Evie," I say.

"Hello, Descendent of Judas."

Its voice is low-pitched, though the odd syllable is high-pitched. It is unlike any sound a human could make.

I stand at the end of the bed and look over the child.

Her arms are covered in cuts. Face covered in bruises. Hair wild and matted and sticking out in all directions.

"I know you are not Evie," I tell it. "But I also know Evie can hear me. Can't she?"

"She's in here, yes."

"Wonderful, then I would like to speak to Evie, if I can. I would like to reassure her that I am here to help. That I know she is suffering, but I will do my best to end that suffering."

The demon chuckles. "You and me both."

I turn to my bag and catch Grace's eye. Her face is a contortion of curiosity and fear. I take out my Dictaphone, place it on the side, and press record.

"So, do you have a name," I ask, "or should I just continue to refer to you as *demon*?"

"Exorcism 101," it replies. "Find out the demon's name. Gain power over it. You know what you're doing."

"Well, do you?"

It sighs and grins wildly. "Isn't this such a cliché?"

"Funny, that's what Evie's mother just said."

"For once, the pitiful slut is right." Grace flinches. "I mean, we've all seen *The Exorcist*, haven't we? Troubled man comes to save troubled girl. It's been done over and over."

"Is that what this is? *The Exorcist*?"

"No. You are not a priest, and I am not a silly little virgin."

"Evie is a virgin, is she not?"

"Not anymore..."

Grace gasps and places both hands over her mouth. It enjoys shocking her.

I reach into my bag and take out a bottle of water. I unscrew the lid and hold it over Evie's head.

"Are you giving me a bath, Descendant of Judas?"

"If that's what you would like to think."

"I could reach out and grab you right now. You know that, right? I could reach out and pull it off."

I ignore it and pour the water over its head.

It lifts its head and feigns enjoyment, allowing it to soak Evie's faded skin.

"Oh, I love me some holy water!" it says.

I screw the top back on the bottle and return it to my bag. I make brief eye contact with Grace as I take out another bottle of water, unscrew the lid, and return to Evie's body.

"Another one?" it says.

I tilt the bottle and pour it over Evie. This time, it makes a *tsst* sound, and the demon darts from the bed to the corner of the room. The water has left a small burn mark on Evie's neck.

"Mo–" Grace says, stepping forward.

"Please," I say, putting my hand out. "Trust me."

It grumbles. At first, I think it's just murmuring. Then I realise it's speaking. But not in English.

I take the Dictaphone and crouch before it.

"Would you like to speak up?" I say.

It continues mumbling, scowling at me, stretching its fingers. It tilts its head to the side. Sticks its tongue out and flicks it up and down. Grace gasps again, but I've seen these intimidation tactics before, and they won't work on me.

It mumbles a little louder, and I can finally recognise the language.

"Is that so?" I say.

It stops talking.

"Any other languages you can speak?"

Its grin returns. It stands, and I edge backwards. Its head tilts further, and its neck makes a cracking sound under the strain. Its arms then join in, twitching in obscure directions, the fingers turning different ways.

"Evie!" Grace cries out.

I put a hand out. "It's doing it on purpose."

"Doing what on purpose? She's hurting herself!"

"She's not doing anything, Grace."

Grace steps from one foot to another, desperate to help, but no idea how she could.

"I hate you, you know," it says, in a different voice.

I recognise that voice.

It's April's voice.

"I really, truly hate you."

I must not let it get to me.

I return to my bag and take out a crucifix. I point it toward the demon, but it is not deterred. It moves toward me, Evie's limbs pointing in directions they shouldn't point.

"I've always hated you."

"Stop it."

My voice sounds pathetic and weak. I reprimand myself for being so easily led. This is what demons do, and I've never let one get to me before.

Then again, I've never faced a demon who can imitate April's voice before. It is a sign of just how embedded this demon is into Evie's skin, and I feel suddenly cold; aware that by backing away, I am letting it win.

So I stand strong.

But it keeps edging forward, its bones making cracking sounds as it advances.

"You could never beat my sweet, sweet Oscar."

"You aren't getting to me," I lie.

"What about now?"

The voice changes again.

It's a voice I haven't heard in years.

I'd almost forgotten how it sounds, but it's unmistakable, and for a moment, I believe that it's really him.

"You've really made a fuck up of yourself, ain't yuh?"

Must not let it get to me.

Must not let it get to me.

Must not let it get to me.

"I left you my car—the one thing I had that wasn't repossessed — and you fucked that up, didn't you?"

"Evie, why are you using language like that?"

I put a hand out to silence Grace.

I'm backing away.

I try not to, but I can't help it.

What if this is actually Dad?

What if this demon has actually brought him into this body with it to torment me?

What if it chose this girl exactly because it is in the flat next to me?

No. Stop it. That's not true. It's just imitating his voice, that's all it is.

It's not real.

It can't be.

"I ought to beat the shit out of you."

"You're not him."

"Do not defy me, boy!"

"Please..."

"Please? You are pathetic..."

I turn to Grace. Tell her I'm done. Blow the candles out, grab my Dictaphone, grab my bag, and leave the room.

Its laughter booms throughout the flat and, despite shutting ourselves in the kitchen, we cannot escape it. It rattles the cupboards, the dishes, the glasses, and it makes my knees go weak, and I can hardly stand.

It's Dad's laughter.

He always laughed at me.

And that's why I hate being laughed at.

Grace stares at me.

"Shall we go to mine?" I suggest, hoping that she will let us escape from this apartment.

"But, Evie..."

"We'll still be able to hear her. Please, I can show you my evidence, and you can decide if you wish to proceed."

"But–"

I decide not to give her a choice. I march through the hallway, out of the door, and hold it open for Grace. She reluctantly follows, and I feel the glares from the lads on the green as Grace locks the door and we enter my flat, where we can still hear Dad's screams.

Eighteen

"What was it you threw on her?" Grace demands as soon as we are in my kitchen.

I put the kettle on, open the cupboard, and take out two tea bags and two mugs.

"Why don't you sit down?"

"What was it? It burnt her. What was in that bottle?"

"Sit down and I will explain."

"I do not want to sit down."

"Fine."

"Was it acid?"

I rub my head. It hurts. I search the draw for some paracetamol, find two pills and swallow them dry.

"Tell me—was it acid you threw on my daughter?"

I reach into my bag and pull out both bottles of water. I unscrew them and turn to her. She flinches as I splash them on her.

She goes to scream, expecting to burn as well.

But she doesn't.

She just has a soggy dressing gown.

"Like I said, why don't you sit down, and I will explain."

Finally, she perches on the edge of the chair at a small table to the side of my kitchen. I place both bottles of water in front of her, and she sniffs them as I finish the cups of tea, bring them over to the table, and sit opposite her.

"It's just water," she says.

"Yep."

"Why did it burn her?"

I lift the first bottle. "This is tap water." I lift the second. "This is holy water—blessed by a priest. To you and I, it will feel no different to tap water. But to a demon..."

She looks confused. I can see the turmoil in her bemused expression. She doesn't know what to think. She doesn't want to believe it, but the evidence is there—the bottle that didn't burn Evie, and the one that did.

"To something impure, it will burn them. To most people who are possessed, it will just cause a little tinge, no more than a flinch. But when you have a demon who has as much control as that one does..."

I lift the cup of tea to my lips and sip it. She stares at her cup, letting her mind fill in the end of my sentence.

"It was a trick," she says. "You did it. I know you did."

I take the Dictaphone from my bag and play it to her. The demon's guttural murmurs repeat themselves to her.

"Do you know what that is?"

"It's just muttering, that's all."

"No, Grace. It's another language."

"Well it's not one I recognise."

"It's probably not one you've ever heard of. It's Wenzhounese."

"What?" She pulls a face.

I sit back and let the Dictaphone play for another few seconds before pausing it.

"It's a Chinese dialect. It's nicknamed the devil's language —but not because of any link to Hell. It's because of how difficult the language is, though demons like to use it because, well, I guess they like irony."

She shakes her head. "How do I know it's—whatever language it is you said?"

"Wenzhounese."

"Whatever. You could be making it up."

I take my phone out and open a translator app, then play the Dictaphone into it. We both watch as it interprets the sound and produces the translation:

I'm going to gut this little piggy she's mine I'm going to eat her soul and spew it into Hell.

"Okay, okay, that's enough."

I stop the translator and put my phone away.

"Tell me," I say, after taking another sip of tea. My head's already feeling better. "Has she ever done anything... inhuman?"

"Like what?"

"Like strength. Has she ever done anything that should be beyond her capability?"

"I... I'm not sure. Maybe."

"Has she ever hurt animals, then wasn't sure why she did it?"

"I... Well... Yes..."

"And has she ever risen off the bed?"

Grace stares at me.

"The doctors may have described it as a seizure, and you may have accepted that, because they are doctors. But you still wondered. They made you question what you saw, but when you think about it, you know what you saw, don't you?"

She gulps.

"Grace, please—do I need to do anything else to convince you?"

Grace says nothing. She stares at her tea, which remains untouched, her hands on her chin, her fingers fiddling with her other fingers. She suddenly cries. She buries her head in her hands, desperate to hide her embarrassment.

I get up and collect a piece of kitchen roll, which I hand to her. She takes it and dabs her eyes. I sit back down, sipping on my tea, looking away from her, not wanting her to feel uncomfortable, knowing that she'll talk when she's ready.

After a few minutes, the crying stops.

"I remember when she was young, younger than she could remember, and her father died. She had only just turned six a week before, and she was playing with a toy jeep in the middle of the living room—she always drove her barbies around in a boy's jeep—and she knew her father was sick, but she didn't know he'd died, not yet, and I had to tell her, and I hated it, I hated seeing the look in her eyes when she heard the news."

She dabs her eyes again, then places the kitchen roll on the table. She places a hand around the mug, but still doesn't drink it.

"It was a few nights later. I was in bed, and I wasn't sleeping. I could never sleep when he went away on business, and so I couldn't sleep now he'd gone away forever. I heard this tiny patter of feet, and the duvet moved, and Evie climbed into bed with me, and she tucked an arm around my waist, and she whispered in my ear. And do you know what she said?"

"What did she say?"

"She said, in the quietest, softest voice—'it's okay, Mummy, that Daddy's gone—because he's in Heaven now, and I know he'll be proud of you.'"

A tear rolls down her cheek. She takes the kitchen roll and starts dabbing her eyes again.

"And that's just Evie, through and through. Even at that

young age, she thought about me over herself. Every other child was always about themselves, about wanting to have the best toy, wanting to make up the rules of a game—Evie was about making sure everyone else was happy, and that they felt good. That's probably why she has no friends now. She's not mean enough."

She huffs. Turns and looks out of the window. The grey clouds part and a bit of sun appears, then disappears seconds later.

"And I know, I mean—I *know*—that is not my daughter. If she's sick, then that sickness is part of my daughter, and I do not believe she is capable of the things she's done, not even when she's sick. Because she doesn't have it in her. There isn't a piece of her that is evil; not even a fingernail."

She leans forward. Takes my hands in hers. Holds them gently. I can feel the moisture of her tears on her fingers.

"Will you help her?" she asks. "Will you get this thing out of her? Will you do that?"

I hesitate. I want to say yes, but it could go wrong, and I don't want to give false hope. But it's tough when she's sitting there, beseeching me to promise her daughter will be okay.

Before I can answer, the wall vibrates under a clatter and a mighty roar comes from the other side.

Grace bows her head and goes to cry again, but I lift her chin up.

"What's inside of her has almost taken over. I have to be honest with you—it would have been ideal to start this battle months ago."

She looks in pain.

"But I promise I will do all I can to get rid of that demon."

"Thank you," she says. "Oh, thank you."

"Don't thank me yet."

She leans back. Takes a moment. Finally lifts the cup of tea and takes a sip. "Its cold," she whispers, before placing it back on the table.

"So when do we start?" she asks.

I look her dead in the eyes. "Now," I say.

"Now?"

"We can't afford to wait any longer. We must begin."

Nineteen

I re-enter the darkness, striding onto the battleground with confidence in my stride and terror in my heart, placing my bag behind me and standing with my feet shoulder width apart.

It sits on the bed, wearing her as a mask. Smiling. Knowing that it is already winning. Knowing it is already strong enough to resist.

Grace stands behind me, and I can sense her wary presence by the door, her fidgeting hands, her weight shifting from one foot to the other.

"Hello," I say, standing at the foot of the bed, the space between us filling with expectation.

It doesn't speak.

"Are you not talking?"

It licks its lips.

"I assume Evie's not coming back now. I assume it's just you."

"It's always me."

Its voice is deep and croaky; nothing like a teenage girl's.

"How about you tell me who you are?"

"I'm Evie."

"I know you are not."

"Yes, I am. I'm the doting little Catholic girl who would never kiss a boy and would never wear a short skirt and would always call that bitch in the corner Mummy."

I hear Grace gasp. I silently wish I'd reminded her not to react.

"Is that what you think of Evie?" I ask.

"I love Evie."

"You do?"

"Very much."

"And this is how you treat someone you love?"

It chuckles. "Would you prefer I beat her? Tell her she's a piece of shit? Kill myself? That's what people do to those they love, don't they?"

I gulp. Tell myself to stop being so weak. Of course it's going to use Dad as ammunition. I need to expect this and stop letting it poke at the open wound.

"Very clever," I say. "Is that all you have? Just insults about my father?"

"Oh, he was a swine, wasn't he?"

Don't react. "I guess he was."

"He would spend time with you in that car, and there'd be flickers of moments where it seemed like he cared, like he didn't hate you—then he'd get drunk, wouldn't he? And he'd whip you with his belt in places that teachers couldn't see."

"You're going to have to do better than that."

"The sad part is—he'd have probably loved you more if you hadn't killed his wife."

Again, this throws me, and I get annoyed with myself.

I reach into my bag and withdraw two sets of handcuffs. I walk slowly around the side of the bed, and its eyes follow me like a creepy painting.

"If you are Evie, perhaps you wouldn't mind if I just restrained you?"

"You sick fuck. This is what you do to teenage girls?"

"Like I said, I–"

Just this once, it uses Evie's voice: "You want to rape me, don't you?"

Grace's hands cover her mouth, and I shoot her a look. I don't know if she'll know what it means, but I'm hoping she will stop giving this thing what it wants.

"If you truly are her, you would let me restrain you."

"You know it won't hold me, don't you? You've done enough of these to know that... I could gut you where you stand."

"Then it won't make any difference to you if I use them."

It doesn't respond. I kneel beside the bed and take her wrist in my hand. The skin is cold in places, and scalding hot in others. There are bumps from cuts along her arm. I place the first handcuff around the wrist and fasten it to the headboard.

I walk around the other side of the bed and do the same, ignoring its triumphant stares, then kneel beside the bed.

It opens its legs and presents Evie's crotch.

"Go on then," it says.

Grace stifles her shock.

"I said go on then—I know you want to. You can tell yourself you don't want to fuck a teenage girl, but we know... We know..."

I take hold of her dress and I lift it up—not to prove the creature right, but to get to Evie's navel. Still, the creature loves it, and begins moaning, gyrating her naked crotch. Crusted blood decorates her inner thigh, and her pubic hair is wild and matted.

"Please..." it groans. "Please touch it... I want you to touch it..."

I ignore it and place my hand on her navel. It writhes around, making a show of its sexual perversion, but I don't pay it any attention. I keep my hand on her navel, and I concentrate.

I bow my head. Close my eyes.

Press harder on her belly.

Wait until the demon's true form manifests in my mind.

"Oh, Moses, oh yes, fuck me like Judas would have..."

I tune it out. Listen to nothing but the erratic breathing in the stomach. I can hear Evie's screams, but I must tune them out, I must focus if I am to see this demon for what it is.

"Fuck me like Judas fucked Jesus... Fuck me like those faggots did... Fuck me, you mother killer, fuck me..."

I see it.

The smoke swirls to create an image in my mind. It comes together, piece by piece.

I see a crown with four horns.

I see a pointed nose.

I see hooked feet.

I see four large, fanged, hooked teeth. Rooster legs.

And I see Evie's soul in its claws.

I know this demon. I've seen it in *The Dictionnaire Infernal*.

I know its name.

I stand. Back away.

It stops wriggling, and it stares at me. Its expression changes. It's no longer playful—it's irate. Furious, even. I see a snarl unlike any I've seen on Evie's face before.

The handcuffs open, and it releases itself, and it rises from the bed, moving toward me.

Grace cannot stifle her shock again. She is in awe. I just find it so very typical.

It's an intimidation tactic that would only throw off an amateur.

Even so, I know that a ferocious bout of rage is imminent.

The demon knows I know.

And it knows its name will give me power.

Which means it will step up its attack. Increase its strength. Make a demonstration of why I should fear it.

"This way," I tell Grace, and I lead her out of the room and into the kitchen.

We can hear it battering the walls, clattering against the floor, screaming with such ferocity that there's no way for us to escape it. The bed shakes and items hit the walls, and I know that the next time we enter that room, its contents will be trashed.

I put the kettle on.

"Have a seat," I tell her.

She sits down, staring ahead, barely moving.

"What is that thing?"

I turn, look her in the eyes, and I say, "Its name is Deumus, and I can tell you everything you need to know about her."

EVIE SPEAKS

He's here to help us.

He's here to destroy us.

I don't think you're right.

I have been alive a lot longer than you have.

But when he touched us, he–

When he touched us, he attacked us.

I really don't think–

Little girl, really, I think you ought to talk less, and listen more.

Mummy used to say that when I was a kid.

I know. That's why I said it. I hoped you would listen.

But–

Enough.

I'm scared.

I said I'm scared.

I thought you loved me.
Love you? I adore you!

Why are you laughing?
I'm laughing at you, you ungrateful little retch.
I'm not ungrateful.
After everything I've done for us.
What is it you've done for us?
I've given you a better experience of life! I used your body to enjoy what the world can offer.
You have defiled my body.
No, you have defiled it by using it as a dormant vessel. I've let us fuck, I've let us hate, and I've let us kill.
Kill?
Yes, kill.
We haven't killed anyone, have we?
Maybe it's best you are quiet.

Please leave.

Did you hear me? I said please leave.

Why won't you talk to—
Shut up.
I'm still in here, you know.
Not for long.
Not for long? This is my body.
Hah!
You can't take my body.
Can't I?
I'll keep shouting.
And with every day I grow stronger, your shouting will become quieter, until you're just a voice in the background. Then one day...

One day what?

I said one day what?

You never did really love me, did you?

This wasn't about love.

You told me it was.. And for what? For this? To take my body?

To just snatch my–
Please tell me, what we're doing with this body that was so great?

It doesn't matter; it was my body.
I think you should be quiet now.

I will not be qui–
I've warned you.
I said I wo—aaaaaaah…

Uuuuuuurgh…

Aaaaargh please stop, please stop, I won't say anything else
I promise just please stop I can't take it I can't aaaaaaargh–

Please don't. No more. No more. Please, I–

Nnnnnnnnuuuuuuuaaaaaaaarrrrrrgggggggghhhhhh

It's too hot. It burns. I can't take anymore, please.

Have you learnt yet?

Fine.

I said have you learnt yet?

I said fine, I've learnt.

I do not think you have.

I hannnnnnnuuuuuuuurrrrraaaaaaaaaagh oh please I have I have please just—just don't—just stop—I can't—please…

Have you learnt now?

There is no us. Not anymore.

Just me, you, and eventually just me.

There is no man to save us. No exorcist. No friendly guy. Just a dope who can't get over his own pointless existence.

You're like him, in a way. Redundant. Pointless. Not deserving of the body you have been given—and should give it to someone who will use it better.

What's the point of life without a little sin, eh?

Heh heh heh.

I noticed you're quiet now. Does this mean you've learnt?

Does it?

...

...

...

Good girl. It'll all be over soon.

For you, anyway.

I promise.

TWENTY

It's hard to decide how much to tell a family member about the demon possessing their loved one.

Often, the truth sounds silly and outlandish. A demon's true form is usually an absurd melding of various animals, and it's hard to believe such creatures exist, even in the pits of Hell. And, even if the family believes what I tell them, does the hideous appearance of a demon possessing their child really comfort them?

I still, however, believe that honesty is an important part of the process. People may not like what they hear, but they deserve to hear the horrible truth rather than a beautiful lie.

I look tentatively at Grace. She sits at the table, hands on her lap, staring at her feet, her eyes wide. She hasn't moved from that position for ten minutes. Perhaps it's shock. Perhaps she just doesn't know what else to do.

"Grace?" I say, and when she doesn't react, I say her name a little louder. "Grace?"

She snaps herself out of it. Her face lifts, and her eyes meet mine, and she looks like she's aged a decade in the past few hours. Her skin has started sagging, her hair looks greyer, and there are coffee stains on her dressing gown.

"Would you like me to tell you about the demon inside of her?" I ask. "Or would you rather not know?"

"I..." Her mouth moves but makes no sound. She shakes her head slightly to herself, briefly closes her eyes, then she looks around before settling her weary eyes back on mine. "Fine."

"Are you sure? We don't have to do this."

"No. Yes, I mean. I am sure. Tell me. I want to know."

I sit forward.

"Okay. It's a female demon and its name is Deumus, though it's also known as Deumo."

"Where did it come from? I mean, where, how, I..."

Her hands are shaking.

"Are you sure you're ready for—"

"Yes, please, just tell me."

"Okay. Most demons were once Heaven's angels, and Deumus is no exception. The earliest reports are of her being worshipped as a goddess by the inhabitants of a place called Calicut in English, but called Kozhikode by the people who live there. It is an Indian city in the State of Karala. It's near a place called Malabar, in the southwest of the Indian continent. That was before she fell into Hell and became a demon."

"I—I don't understand. She's from India?"

"No, Grace, she was worshipped in India many centuries ago. She was originally a warrior goddess who defended the righteous from another demon. She was first discovered to be tormenting people in the western world when a group of Portuguese sailors came across her near the coast of Malabar. That's when she spread her torment to the west. Of course, this happened a long time ago."

She stares at me. Her eyes twitch. Her breathing is slightly erratic. But she seems calm.

"There is a book called The Dictionnaire Infernal, written in 1818 by a French occultist called Jacques Albin Simon Collin de Plancy, which is where Deumus's appearance is recorded."

I wait for a reaction. Her face looks empty. Like all emotions have faded away from her.

"Would you like to know what she looks like?"

She nods, faintly.

"She wears a crown over four horns. Has four large, hooked teeth. A pointed nose. Rooster legs. In pictures, they normally show her holding a soul between her claws. I imagine that, once she has removed a soul from its body, she devours it, before digesting it and sending it to Hell."

I wonder why I just gave her that bit of information. She didn't need to know that.

"I..." She goes to speak, then doesn't.

She stands, suddenly. Hobbles to the kitchen sink. Opens a drawer and removes a pack of cigarettes.

"I didn't know you smoked," I say.

"I don't. I quit."

She takes a cigarette out and places it between her lips. She takes a lighter and tries to lift it, but her arms are shaking too much, and her hands are quivering, and she can't keep it still enough to light the tip.

She huffs, drops her hands, then tries again, lifting her trembling arms.

I take the lighter from her and hold it at the end of the cigarette until it's lit. She takes a breath, coughs, and I place the lighter back in the drawer. I place a hand on her back and help her back to her seat.

She takes another drag, then holds the cigarette between her fingers which can't stay still.

"Have you ever fought this demon before?" she asks.

"This one? No."

"Have you fought others as strong as this one?"

"It's not necessarily the strength of the demon, but the time they've accrued in the body that gives them strength. The longer they are there, the stronger they get."

She raises her eyebrows and takes another drag on her cigarette.

"But I have fought demons before," I add. "Strong ones. Ones that have been there for a while."

"And did you win?"

I go to answer, then don't. I don't want to lie. I don't want to give her unrealistic expectations. But I also worry that the wrong sentence may be enough to push her over the edge.

"Most of them," I answer.

"Most?"

"Yes, most."

"And the ones that you lost—what happened? Did the victim have to live with this thing inside of them forever?"

If only they got off that lightly.

"No."

"Then what happened?"

"I really don't think you want to–"

"Tell me. I want to be prepared for the worst."

I bite my lip. Sigh. Readjust myself in the seat.

"The girl killed her parents, and then herself. Her soul would have then been sent to Hell to suffer an eternity of torment."

She doesn't react. Her face remains stone cold, and I think I've done the right thing in answering her honestly. Then she covers her face with her hands, the end of the cigarette poking between thick strands of straggly hair, and cries silently, her whole body wobbling under the strength of her tears.

I am tempted to put an arm around her, but I don't.

It's not what she needs.

She needs to see this through. Endure the pain. Process the information, however much it hurts.

Except, I can't just watch her, so I eventually speak.

"I have defeated most demons I've faced," I offer.

She keeps her face covered. Doesn't look up.

"Normally I get them in the early stages, and it's not quite as tough, but this isn't the first time I've fought..."

I stop talking. I'm not helping.

I go to collect some kitchen roll for her, but there is only a cardboard tube.

So I just sit, and I wait, and I let her do what she needs to do.

Then a huge thud from Evie's room forces her to lift her head.

"It's okay, it's going to make noises to—"

Another thud.

Followed by another, then another.

They are footsteps. Heavy, like a sasquatch walking across her room. Then the door creaks open slightly, and the artificial light from the hallway illuminates a hand reaching out of it. The nails are broken, and the skin is cracked.

Then the door is full open, and it stands there.

And I know exactly what it's doing.

It sees me as a threat, so it will not wait any longer.

It's bringing the war to me.

Twenty-One

"Oh, Evie," Grace moans upon seeing her daughter's state. Somehow, Evie has deteriorated further. Whilst she was already demented and hideous, there was still a part of her that kept a slight hint of humanity.

That is gone now.

In every step, its knees bend to the side, and its arms click out of place, and its head hangs low, and her hair, which used to be light, is now dark and blackened. Its eyes, black and fully dilated, lock onto mine as it limps forward. The constant contortions of her body are painful and unnatural, but that won't bother the demon—the demon can give Evie the job of dealing with the pain while it focuses on everything else.

"Moses... Iscariot..."

Its voice is a husky whisper; a deep, drawn-out wheeze from somewhere deep inside.

I stand. Take a crucifix from my bag and clutch it.

"I know your name, demon," I tell it.

It hobbles into the kitchen, edging toward me. Every ominous step fills me with dread, and I don't know why—I have fought demons before. Not alone, but still, this is nothing new. So why am I intimidated by this one?

I straighten my back. Clench my jaw. Try to show this thing nothing but strength.

"Moses... Iscariot..."

"That is my name. And yours is Deumus. And now I know your name, you must realise, I have the–"

"Colin... Iscariot..."

"What?"

Colin?

That was Dad's name. Why is she—

"He's here... With us..."

He's not. It's lying.

I told Grace not to listen to it; I must do the same.

I hold the crucifix toward it, gripping tightly.

"When time began, the word was there, and the word was face to face with God–"

"He... Wants... To... Talk... With you..."

I shake myself out of it. Glance over my shoulder. Grace is pressed against the far wall.

The demon moves to within a few steps toward me. I don't back up. I will not show this thing weakness.

"All things came into being through Him, and without Him there came to be not one thing as–"

"You... Can... See... Him..."

I look around, expecting to see Dad, then scald myself again for listening to it.

"The light shone in the darkness, and the darkness did not lay hold of it–"

"He... Still... Hates... You..."

It halts in front of me. Inches away. It stinks. Not just of body odour and garlic and decaying eggs and expired milk and putrid fruit—but of evil, too. You can always smell evil. It's like shit and rotten strawberries.

It lifts its head. Eyes meet mine. There is a glimmer of red in the black pupils. Its mannerisms are stiff and irregular, just like every other demon I've fought.

"He was in the world, and the world came to be through Him–"

It shoves his open palm against my heart and sends something through me, like a jolt of electricity, a burst of flames, shooting up and down my muscles, stiffening and relaxing them at the same time.

My body shakes.

My mind fails to make sense.

My thoughts are bizarre, like the thoughts you have just before you fall asleep. Everything is right but also wrong. It makes sense whilst making no sense at all.

My body convulses, then drops to the floor, and when I wake up, I am no longer in Grace's kitchen.

I am in a garage.

It's smaller than I remember it—but I do remember it. Boxes of Mum's stuff still fill the corners and line the walls. The 1965 Ford Mustang is there, the hood still open from when Dad was working on it the other day. The rain outside batters against the garage door with such force it feels like it's going to give way.

I remember that rain. I've never known rain like it.

I've seen storms before, but nothing has ever bombarded the garage door like the rain on that night.

"Oh, no..."

I remember what day it is.

I turn around. Look up.

A noose hangs from the wooden beams in the garage's roof by a triple knot. A chair below it.

"Please, no..."

The door that leads from the garage to the house opens and closes behind me. I turn away, not wanting to see this. I never actually witnessed this happening. I just found him when I came home. I was at a friend's house, watching *Looney Tunes.* My friend's mum cooked us burgers with sliced cheese and gherkins.

I haven't eaten another burger or gherkin since that day.

I've always wondered how Dad was when he approached that noose. Was he confident in what he was doing? Was he crying? Was he having second thoughts, or was he so sure of what he wanted that he never looked back?

I am tempted to look at him. To turn around and see. But how do I even know this is real?

I give in. I turn around. Dad is standing with his back to me, and a box of Mum's stuff is open. He holds a photo frame before him.

We never had photos of Mum in the house. Not a single one.

We had photos of Elvis Presley and Frank Sinatra and The Sex Pistols on the wall—but we never had a photo of someone we actually knew.

He bows his head. His strong, sturdy body slumps in a way that I don't recognise. He was always so domineering, so forceful. Always the alpha male. To see him so weak is a shock that I can't quite adjust to.

He puts the photo frame back and closes the box. He turns to the noose and strides toward it, closing his eyes briefly as he gathers the strength to do what he wants to do.

"Dad..."

He doesn't react.

"Dad, can you hear me?"

Nothing.

"Dad!"

I bow my head. Run my hands through my hair. Then look up. I don't want to watch, though I'm unable to do anything but.

He steps onto the chair. Takes the noose. Puts it around his neck.

But he doesn't kick the chair away.

He stays there. Considering it.

And it seems like he's having second thoughts.

And, even though I know how this turns out, I feel hope that he won't do it. He's thinking about it, and he's thinking long and hard, and there are all kinds of pained expressions going across his face, but he's still standing there.

He takes a deep breath, holds it, then releases it.

Then he says, softly, "No."

And he seems to look in my direction as he says, "I can't do this to you..."

And he goes to take the noose off, and my heart races, and my God he will not go through with it, he will not ruin my life, he's going to make amends, treat me better, be the man he wants to be, and–

We are not alone.

There is something else.

It's *her*.

"What are you doing here?"

She's behind him. Hair over her face. Crooked body. Contorted limbs.

Dad goes to remove the noose, but she grabs the rope and tightens it around his neck, and he can't remove it. He struggles hard, but she is too strong.

She holds his hands behind his back so he can't stop her.

Then she kicks the chair out.

"No!"

And she watches me, grinning, licking her lips as I witness Dad suffocate. He wheezes and whimpers and gasps and cries, but nothing helps; he is dying, and it is painful, and he can't do anything about it.

I go to look away, but something stops me. My head is held in place. Forcing me to watch.

It's taking so long.

I didn't realise his death would be like this. I thought it would be quicker.

Maybe I can stop it.

Maybe I can push her away.

I charge forward, toward her, and I dive on her, and I take her to the floor, and we land on the solid tiles of Grace's kitchen, and I am on top of Evie's body and Deumus is laughing and Grace is pushing herself against the far wall with her hands over her mouth.

I quickly climb off.

The demon lies on the floor, smirking up at me.

I look at Grace.

And I try not to cry, but a tear trickles down my cheek, despite my determination not to let it.

Dad would have told me to grow up and stop being such a little bitch.

He said men don't cry.

He said that men fight.

But I guess I'm just not a man, then. I guess I'm still that boy who found his father's body hanging from a wooden beam in the garage.

"I can't..." I tell Grace, not knowing I'm saying it. "I can't..."

"What?"

"I can't help you..."

Grace's face is gripped with pain. "What do you mean, you can't help us?"

The demon still looks up at me. It's too strong. It's got too much of a grip on her and me. It knows too much.

I can't do anything here.

I'll just rile the demon and Evie will suffer more.

I back up, edging toward the door.

"Where are you going?" Grace asks.

I run into the hallway.

"Mo! Please, come back!"

I open the front door.

And I pause.

And I ask myself what the hell I'm doing.

"Please!"

But I can't.

I just can't.

So I close the door, run into my flat, and lock the door and bolt it and even put a chair up against it.

Then I run into the bedroom and pull the duvet over me, hiding from the monsters like I did when I was a child.

Running and hiding.

It's how I survived as a kid.

And I guess it's how I'm going to survive now.

I stay here all night, and eventually silence settles in. There is no banging against the wall. No roaring. No screams.

I guess it doesn't need to do that anymore.

There's no point trying to dominate your opponent when they've already won.

Deumus Speaks

It's finally quiet.

She's stopped her incessant chatter and her relentless moaning. Her head fills with nothing but my thoughts. She is distant, hidden away, gone to a part of her body where she can wither away and die.

It won't be long now.

And your saviour?

Your wonderful exorcist?

I've never known anyone so easily deterred. All you need to do is show them a glimpse, that's all it takes—just a glimpse—and they can't take anymore.

I've never found it difficult to figure out which wound to pour salt into.

Of course, it's changed over the years.

Centuries ago, it was famine. A man in poverty, stealing bread for his child, feared that he would be caught and subsequently stoned to death. A rich man would fear that his daughter was promiscuous, and therefore undesirable for a potential husband. A woman would fear that she'd give birth to an illegitimate child and be sent to an asylum.

Today's fears are so much more... how do I put it... meaningless.

They are pointless worries. People don't worry about poverty or famine or survival anymore. They worry about whether their phone is charged. Whether they will look bad on social media. Whether their daddy was too mean to them as a child.

People are far easier to manipulate these days. It is much simpler to penetrate someone's soul when all their worries are immaterial.

And Evie...

What can I say about this girl?

I love a good Catholic girl.

I love them virgin and pure. Desperate not to touch a man before marriage. Desperate to obey strict rules that make them such a tediously dull person.

At least drunks have decent stories to tell. This girl? She didn't even have a friend to tell a story to if she had one.

She was so lonely that she was thrilled to have me in her life.

She was so naïve she believed I was a friend.

She was so desperate for affection she believed I loved her.

And where is she now?

Somewhere in here. With me. Hiding away so I can't hurt her anymore.

Though sometimes I still do, just for fun.

Nnnnnnyaaaaaaaargh.

Heh.

It's not that a human has to be weak, but it's so much easier if they are.

Aaaaaargh please stop please stop I'm staying quiet I am please just don't.

See that?

She's begging to be left alone in her own body.

I have control.

It's power you can't possibly comprehend.

There's no escape from me. I have invaded her head, and anytime I feel like it, I just...

Aaaaargh God please stop please...

Hear that?

She's sobbing.

She's nothing now.

No, she was nothing before.

She's become less than that.

I can feel her soul in my palm. It's squishy and covered in bruises, like a rotten banana. Sometimes I lick it so she can feel my coarse tongue.

Sometimes I just squeeze it to make her scream.

Please… I can't take anymore…

Hear that?

It's a glorious symphony.

It's power in its most glorious form.

And I think these lamentations can stop now, can't they?

She has nothing left to say, and I have nothing more I need to say.

Her saviour has gone.

Her mother is broken.

And Evie's soul has almost faded.

It has never been clearer when I have won.

Twenty-Two

I lay on the sofa. Staring at nothing. My leg dangles over the armrest. My hand drops to the floor and lands in something soft and wet. Maybe I spilled my beer. I don't know.

The ceiling spins and loses focus.

At some point, I fall asleep. I don't know how. It doesn't last long. I wake up sweating, images of Dad scarred into the back of my eyes.

His body was limp by the time I found him. He'd been hanging there for a few hours. His face was empty in a way I couldn't understand at such a young age. I thought it was the worst thing I'd ever seen.

Until today.

When I watched him suffocate.

Was it real? Did I actually witness Dad hanging himself? Or was it just a hallucination induced by a powerful demon?

Stop it, for fuck's sake. I can't... I just can't...

I allow my eyes to close again, wondering if I will return to sleep. Dad's face multiplies, over and over, until there are too many of him, stepping onto the chair, placing nooses around his necks, and I sit up. Rub my eyes and rest my head in my hands.

What time is it?

The dim light of the television reveals a blank screen, and I realise that whatever channel I was watching has gone off air. I don't remember turning it on. I search for the remote, unable to find it on the arms of the sofa, on the floor, or in the mess shoved into the corner of the room. Eventually, I find it down the side of the sofa. I press the i button, hoping it will tell me what time it is, but the television doesn't respond. I remember the batteries are almost gone. I take the back off, rub them, then press the button as hard as I can until something comes up.

It's gone three in the morning.

Is that it?

I was hoping I would close my eyes, then open them again, and it would be morning, and this night would be over, and I can leave my flat to get more beer.

I stand. Beer cans surround my feet. My legs are stiff. I stretch my back, hoping to bring a bit of life to my body. I hobble to the kitchen and open the fridge. There's a pack rotten mushrooms and a single can of supermarket own-brand lager.

I take the beer, open it, and neck it down. My throat feels dry, and it makes the beer taste so much better.

I look down at the can. Being supermarket own-brand, the can is plain. No claims to be the best lager, or that it's refreshing, or that it's even any good. Just white with a few ingredients written on the side.

I take another swig.

Three forceful knocks pound against my front door.

I drop my head. Dammit. I told Grace I couldn't do anything. I want to be left alone. I'm just going to make things worse.

This demon has won. There's no point trying to fight it.

I gulp down another large mouthful of beer. It tastes plain. Like it's just alcohol and yeast. But if it helps me sleep, I'll take it.

Those knocks again. Even louder. Even more forceful.

I slam my hands on the kitchen side. Shake my head. Get it in your head, would you? I'm not good enough for this.

I'm not good enough for anything.

I ignore it. Finish the beer. Crush the can, then drop it. It makes me feel more manly. Which is pathetic, I know.

Those knocks come again. More of them this time—five or six.

I punch the wall and march through the corridor, stumbling a little. If she won't piss off, then I will have to tell her in no uncertain terms to piss off. I'm too tired and too drunk for this.

I swing the door open.

It's not Grace.

"All right, mate?"

There's nothing nice in the way he calls me *mate.*

It's the group of lads that firebombed Dad's car. The ones that Grace saved me from when they were beating me up. The ones who hang around on the green, drinking and smoking weed, decreasing society's average IQ.

"What can I do for you?"

"We heard you been hurting the girl next door," the one to my left says. He wears a white vest to show off his gangly arms.

"What?" I say.

"I said, we heard you been hurting that girl next door."

"No, I haven't."

"Well, you been spending a fair bit of time in her company, innit?" says the one to my right. The one with the shaved head and the tracksuit bottoms halfway down his arse.

"It's not like that."

"Not like what?"

"You a fucking paedo, mate?" says the third one, stood directly in front of me; the one with a piercing in his eyebrow and a matching grey tracksuit.

"No, I am not–"

"'Cause we don't want paedos hanging around here, you get me?" White Vest says.

"An' we think you ought to find somewhere else to live, innit?" Eyebrow Piercing says.

"I am not a–"

"What else you spending all that time with her for?" White Vest again.

"We seen Grace and that. She looks like shit. She's all stressed 'cause her daughter's ill, an' you are taking advantage of that, ain't you?"

"No, I am not. Now, if you don't mind, I don't need to justify myself to you."

I go to close my door. White Vest puts a hand out to block it. I try to force it closed, but he's too strong.

"I think you do, blood," he says.

"Let go of my door." I try to sound forceful and confident, but I just sound weak and annoyed.

"I think we need to show you what we do to paedos who abuse girls around here."

"You know she's sixteen, right?" I say. "Even if I was abusing her, she's too old for it to be paedophilia."

If I was abusing her?

That was the wrong thing to say.

I'm an idiot.

I try to close my door again, but Eyebrow Piercing grabs the collar of my shirt and drags me out of the flat. He shoves me on the floor, and I try to get up, but he pushes me back down with the muddy side of his boot.

"I haven't hurt her," I insist. "I–"

A boot comes from behind me—from White Vest, I guess —and slams on my forehead, smacking my head against the solid surface.

An immense headache starts, and everything goes fuzzy.

Then a boot lands in my belly, and I am winded, and I struggle to breathe.

Then another on my shin. On my side. On my neck.

I am too drunk for this. I try to move onto my front and crawl away, but one of them just drags me down and punches me, hard, to the side of my head.

One of them picks me up and presses me against the railings. They all pound on me, punches to my chest, my head. Heels to my kneecap. Fists to my throat.

I drop to the floor and feel the warmth of my blood as I land in it.

My entire body throbs, pulsating under the pain.

The agony fires through my body.

Then a boot lands against my forehead and hits my head against the floor, and I am knocked out.

Twenty-Three

I come around in flashes...

...

...

...

A blow to my head, and another, repetitive, like a metronome, a bout of pain in rhythmic bursts...

...

...

...

A pair of shoes passing my face. Quick steps running away. A voice filled with panic. Doors opening...

...

...

...

A man in green dives to his knees. A woman in green dives to her knees. They are on either side of me. They are talking quickly. I hear words like *now* and *we need to* and *life threatening*...

...

...

...

I'm travelling. There are sirens. Something is attached to my arm. Is it an IV? I ask questions and I'm told something. Not sure what...

...

...

...

Artificial lights overhead. Passing quickly. Long and thin. Plain ceiling. Sterile walls...

...

...

...

Beeping. Quick beeping. Panic. People rushing around me. A blur of bodies. Hysteria. I lift my hand. At least, I think I do. It doesn't seem to move...

...

...

...

Everything's calm. I look up. Is that April?

...

...

...

Is that April's face?

...

...

...

"I love you..."

...

...

...

April...

...

...

...

"Let me go! Get off me! Get off!"

...

...

...

Something enters my arm. My muscles relax.

...

...

...

And then the glimpses stop, and I'm just a body, lying in a bed, waiting to wake up.

TWENTY-FOUR

My eyes open. There are two windows. Light bursts through them. I'm in a bed.

The beep of a machine echoes my pulse.

I look around. I'm in a hospital. There is a curtain around half of my bed. The walls are white. There is an IV stand next to me, and the tube leads to my hand.

I try to sit up, but it hurts too much, and a voice tells me to stay where I am.

I know that voice.

"April…"

I turn to my right. There she is. Sat in a chair with a book on her lap—a worn copy of something by Richard Matheson. She looks at me, and her smile makes me feel lighter. She dresses just as she always does—baggy jeans, purple hair, bracelets around her wrists. I think she has a new tattoo on her arm. Possibly another Tim Burton character.

"April?"

"Hey," she says, her voice quiet and soothing, which I appreciate—my head is pounding.

"What are you doing here?"

I hate that it's the first thing out of my mouth.

I could tell her how much I've missed her, how messed up things have been, how much my life sucks now...

But instead, I ask her an accusatory question about why she's here.

It doesn't seem to bother her. She just smiles and answers, "I'm still down as your emergency contact."

I nod. Stupid me.

"Would you rather I go?" she asks.

I gaze at her. My body aches, my sore muscles throb, and the catheter is uncomfortable.

"No," I say. "Please stay."

"You did well to stay hidden, though. We had no idea where you were."

"That was the point."

"Well, remind me never to play hide and seek with you. I'd never find you again."

I chuckle. Typical April, always making horrible situations feel bearable.

My memory hits me like a brick to the face. I have a vague recollection of why I am here—a few images of those three guys banging on my door, accusing me of abusing Evie, and beating the shit out of me. The recollections hurt my head.

"How long have I been out?" I ask, fearing that I've been comatose.

"About half a day," she says, and I breathe a sigh of relief. "I mean, you came around a couple of times. Once in the ambulance, once when we were here—but you wouldn't stay still, so the doctor gave you a sedative."

"A sedative?"

"You were really uncooperative—I don't think he had much choice."

I roll my head back. This pillow is big and comfortable. I

lift my arms, which ache like hell, and run my hands over my face.

"Where's Evie?"

"Evie?"

"The girl next door."

"I don't know."

My head is pounding. It slowly dawns on me that I've lost. That Evie is damned. That I've let yet another person down.

"I should probably let the doctor know you're awake," April says as she gets up. "The police will probably want to speak to you."

"The police?"

"Yeah—they caught the guys who did it. They weren't tough to find, I don't think. They'd just recently installed some new CCTV. Sounds like most people on the block recognised the men."

She goes to open the door and I raise my arm weakly to stop her, which she doesn't notice.

"April, don't. Just stay."

She pauses and looks back at me. "But you might be concussed, we need to–"

"Yes, fine, in a minute. Let me just... I don't know. Just hang on."

April reluctantly returns to her seat. She watches me tentatively, like I'm a bomb waiting to explode.

"I think it will be pretty easy to charge the guys who did this," she says. "The police were pretty confident that—"

"I don't care. It'll just be a waste of time. Besides, I deserve it."

"You do?"

"Yes. I tried to help a girl, and I only made things worse."

She leans forward. "Tell me about this girl, Mo."

I consider whether to tell her, but she's probably the best

person to tell. I open my mouth and unload the story of the past few weeks on her.

When I'm done, she sits for a moment in silent contemplation before speaking again.

"Do you want some help with her?"

"Do I want help? Are you not going to..."

"This is your case, Mo. It's up to you."

"But I'm not a Sensitive anymore."

"You will always be a Sensitive, Mo, it makes no difference whether you are with us or not. You can run away all you like; this gift will always follow you. You'll always see it in people, feel it when you walk past it. It isn't something you just quit."

"But I want to quit. It's not a gift, it's a burden."

"It's an opportunity."

"Not for a bum like me."

"A bum? Mo, you're not a bum. You're one of the bravest people I know. Now, do you want our help or not?"

I watch her for a moment. She looks healthy. Vibrant. Full of vigour. Even after all the people she's lost, and the pain this war has put her through, she is still enthusiastic about it.

I had one bad day, and I packed it in.

That's why she is so much better than I am.

"There's only one thing I want from you, April," I say. "And we both know I'm not going to have it."

April sighs. "I'm just not ready to–"

"Yeah, I know. You don't need to tell me again."

A silence passes between us. The first awkward one. I don't like it, and I wish she would leave.

But she doesn't.

Instead, she fetches the doctor, who comes in and talks to me about the damage that's been done. I don't listen much. I gather that it's all stuff that will fix itself, and I just need to rest in hospital for another few days. The police come in after the doctor to take my statement and reassure me the guys have been charged, though I don't really care.

Throughout the entire ordeal, April remains in her seat, watching without saying a word.

By the time they are all gone, I feel exhausted. Night time has arrived, and I am struggling to stay awake.

"I guess I better go," April says, standing up and putting her bag over her shoulder.

"I guess this is goodbye, then."

April laughs. "I meant to go back to my hotel. I'm not going anywhere, Mo."

"Really, you don't need to–"

"Don't argue. I'm not going to let you sit in this bed on your own for the next few days."

She steps forward and places her hand on mine. Her skin is soft and mine is rough and coarse. As soon as she makes contact, I feel suddenly alive again.

The beeping of my heart monitor gets quicker, and she takes her hand away.

"I'll see you in the morning," she says, then turns and leaves, and I keep watching the door long after she's gone.

And I fall back asleep.

And, just as she promised, she is there next to me in the morning when I wake up.

Sometimes we talk. Sometimes she reads as I sleep. Sometimes she does some cross-stitching—something I never knew she did. And sometimes she pops out to get me food that's better than the hospital provides.

But she doesn't leave.

Unlike me.

She's good like that, you see.

It's the kind of person she is, and the kind of person I will never be.

Twenty-Five

The morning in the hospital turns into afternoon, which turns into night, and I start to feel that I am a burden. There are people weaker than me who are in much greater need of this hospital bed. The doctor insists, however, that there is damage to a few of my blood vessels and muscles he wants to check on, as well as doing a few more tests for brain damage before I go—just to be sure.

But I know I don't have brain damage. I mean, my head was stomped on pretty badly, and I have a constant pounding headache that won't go away, but I'll be fine. And I want to leave.

There's just a single thought that makes me hesitate.

April.

Will she go back home? Will we go back to never seeing each other?

It is both beautiful and agonising to be with her. Both wonderful and painful. She is the wound I keep picking at.

After joining me for a walk around the hospital to prove to the doctors that I am fine, April and I return to the cubicle I hope to leave soon.

Grace sits on the edge of the chair.

My body stiffens. She's the last person I wanted to see.

She isn't wearing her dressing gown anymore. In fact, she is wearing a suit—with a blazer, a knee-length skirt and a blouse. It looks completely out of place on her. It is crumpled and creased, and poorly fitted, and does not detract from the heavy bags beneath her eyes, but I suppose it's an improvement.

"Grace?" I say, and she stands, her hands nervously fidgeting. April helps me to the bed, and I sit on the edge.

"April, this is Grace. Grace, this is April." I meet Grace's feeble eyes with mine. "She's a Sensitive. A far better one. Maybe she can help you."

Grace looks weak. Her skin wraps tightly around her bones. She opens her mouth, and a croak comes out. I can tell she is desperate to say something, but I can also tell it is destroying her to say it.

"I can't help you, Grace, I–"

"She's gone."

It takes a moment for me to understand what she's talking about.

"What do you mean, she's gone?"

"Evie's gone. They took her away."

"Who took her away?"

Grace's lip trembles and she struggles not to crumble. April stands beside me, showing the kind of expression one should show in this situation—concern, caring, an eagerness to help. I rub my head and wonder why I can't look like that.

"Soc– soc–" Her face breaks as she forces herself to say it. "Social services."

She buries her head in her hands and cries. April takes a packet of tissues from her bag and hands one to her, then strokes her back.

"Why did they take her?"

"Those guys who hurt you, I think they phoned them, or someone did, I don't know. They showed up and saw her."

"How bad was she?"

She struggles to speak. "She'd... Weed herself... Scars down her arms... They said she was malnourished... They said it looked like a case of neglect. I have to go to a hearing."

Ah, that would explain the suit.

"So where is she now?"

"They said they've put her in temporary foster care. I can't... I need her back..."

I look at April. Whilst I am concerned for Grace, and for Evie, my immediate thought is with the foster parents. They don't know what they are dealing with.

And their lives will be in grave danger.

From the look on April's face, I can tell she's concerned too.

Even so, I hesitate. I know I should be courageous, and help Grace, and help Evie—but I'm a coward.

Although, not according to April.

And, as I stare into her eyes, I see myself how she sees me. As a troubled man. Not a lost cause, but someone who's worth sticking around for. And I can't decide whether she's right, or whether she's a fool, but it makes me want to be the person she thinks I am.

"Do you know where this foster home is, Grace?"

"Yes, they say I'm allowed supervised visits on a weekly basis while the foster parents watch..."

She trails off.

"I need some clothes," I tell April. "I can't leave like this."

"Are you helping me?" Grace says, her wobbly voice showing hints of optimism.

"Grace, your daughter..."

I don't know how to say this. Man, this is tough.

"Evie might be beyond saving. But the foster parents she's

with... We've known people who are this far along with demonic possession who go on to commit appalling acts toward others. We've witnessed... murder."

"You think Evie might kill them?"

"No, I think Deumus might."

I stand. My legs still ache, but my mind is full of resolve. April reaches into her bag and pulls out a t-shirt and jeans.

"Where did you get them from?"

"I went back to your flat and got some for you."

How did I ever get by without this woman?

"April—can you get in touch with the foster parents?"

"And tell them what?"

Good point.

"What are you going to do?" Grace asks, and I look from her weary face to April's expectant expression.

And I sigh.

Once again, I am being pulled back into a battle I thought I'd left.

"We are going to take your daughter from her foster home," I announce. "Then we are going to try another exorcism."

"But you said she's too far along—what if it doesn't work?"

I look at April. We hold each other's stare. There's no point being anything but honest.

"Then hopefully we'll be able to push the demon aside long enough for you to say goodbye."

Before she can object any further, I remove my gown and get dressed, not caring whether they see me—though I catch April's face in the window's reflection as she looks away.

Once I am done, I turn to find April staring at me.

"We need the church's help, Mo."

"No, we don't–"

"You think the foster parents will let Evie go? You think if we manage to take her, that the police won't come after us? We need the church's power—it's the only way."

I hesitate. I know she's right. There is a teenage girl suffering the kind of torment that people struggle to recover from, and we don't have time to argue.

I walk out, and their footsteps follow me.

TWENTY-SIX

We climb into the back of a car that Grace tells us she borrowed from her sister. The inside smells like children. There are bits of crisps dug into the cracks between the seats, and it makes a horrible churning sound every time Grace changes gear.

We sit in silence as she drives. The radio hisses in the background, but nobody else seems to notice. April's hand rests in the space between us. I imagine what it would be like to reach over and hold it. Whether she would recoil and scowl, or whether she would turn and smile. I've dreamt of doing such things, which makes me feel pathetic. What kind of guy fantasises about holding hands?

After ten or fifteen minutes, Grace pulls up outside a large family home. Two hanging baskets on either side of the front door, full of colour. The garden path is lined with flowers. A sparkling clean people carrier sits in the driveway. It's the kind of family home Grace wants to give Evie, but can't. It must be hard feeling like your daughter is better off in another person's house—like she would have a better life with these foster parents. I see it in her face, the longing look, the tearful eyes.

I reach my hand forward and place it on her shoulder.

"We'll get her back," I tell her.

Grace bows her head and says nothing. I turn to April. A streetlamp lights half her face.

"Let's go through to the garden, see if there's a way to climb in," I say, then turn to Grace. "You stay here—and keep the engine running."

Grace stares into her lap and gives a faint nod.

April and I leave the car and sneak around the side of the house. As quietly as I can, I unbolt the garden gate, and we creep into the garden. There is a pond surrounded by plant life, a pristine wooden bench, and a trellis fence up the side of the walls covered in green leaves.

There are two upstairs windows. Both are open, but we don't know which room Evie is in—if she's even in either of them.

"Come on," I say. I take hold of the trellis fence and climb upwards. April follows.

When I reach the top, I check my balance, holding precariously onto the fence with one hand, and pull the nearest open window wider. I peek inside.

A man and a woman sleep in the bed, and I flinch out of the way.

"The foster carers," I whisper to April, who peers into another window.

We both climb across the fencing, and my arms wobble, and I tell myself to get a grip, and we reach the last window, and I look inside.

And I see it.

Sitting cross-legged on the bed.

Staring at me.

As if it's waiting.

As if it's expecting us.

I open the window as wide as it will go, reach an arm over

the windowsill, and drag myself in. I fall to the floor, causing a thud, and I freeze, waiting for footsteps from another room.

I hear nothing but silence.

I push myself to my feet, brush leaves off my clothes, and stand in front of Evie's body. How anyone can think this is still a sweet, sixteen-year-old girl is beyond me. There is nothing resembling human left.

When April reaches my side and casts her eyes over it, I feel her body tense.

"Wow..." she whispers. "This is really bad..."

We both stare at it, waiting for it to move.

But it doesn't.

Not at all.

It just stares at us.

"How do we do this?" I ask her.

She shrugs. "I don't think we can do it without making a noise."

I step toward it. It stinks. Its grin widens. I stop. Watching it, wary.

"What are you doing?" I ask it.

It doesn't reply.

Screw it. I step toward it, open my arms, ready to pick Evie's body up, and it screams with a high-pitched, screeching wail. And it doesn't stop. It continues screaming, voices of different pitches combining into a shrieking yet guttural howl.

Movements come from down the hall. The thudding of feet on the floor as someone gets out of bed. The carers are up.

I look at April, and she immediately tells me, "Grab her— I'll take care of the foster parents."

"But you'll get arrested."

She smiles at me like I'm a child who just said something stupid. "It's fine—the Church won't be far away. They will sort it out, I just need to stall them for a few minutes."

Of course, the Church will sort it out.

I try not to get annoyed. I don't have time. I go to grab Evie's body, and it pushes me away, swiping her long, filthy fingernails at my face, and swinging its legs at my belly.

I throw my body on it, pinning it to the bed. It wriggles and squirms and swings its elbows at my ribs and its nails scrape across my cheek and draw blood.

I push all my body weight down on her, wrap my arms around her waist, and pick her up. It kicks and thrashes and swings her arms backwards and hits me over and over, but I do my best to endure it, carrying her down the stairs, almost stumbling under the weight of the battering body.

April stays upstairs, and I hear a man shouting, then I hear April's voice, then all I can hear is the demon screaming in my ear.

Whilst keeping both arms wrapped around Evie, I stretch my fingers to the keys, unlock the front door, and carry her down the driveway.

An elbow lands against my head. It makes me dizzy for a moment, and I drop her, but manage to grab her ankle and stop it from getting away. I dive on top of her, wrap my arms around her waist, and pick it back up.

As I approach the car, I make eye contact with Grace in the mirror.

"Go! Go!" I shout as I shove Evie in the backseat and get in, holding her down with my body weight.

TWENTY-SEVEN

Grace swings the car around the corner, braking suddenly for a bike, then accelerating past it.

"Grace!" I shout over the constant moaning. "Drive slowly—we don't want to attract attention!"

"Where should I go?"

That's a good question. Where should we go?

I try to think for a moment, peering down upon the writhing body I keep desperately pinned to the backseat.

"How far away is the church?"

"About twenty minutes, maybe? There's one just past the woods."

Twenty minutes of having to keep it still and contained?

Hell, I can't think of anywhere better for us to go.

"Fine, go there," I say, and I turn my full attention to Deumus.

It kicks at the window, swings its arms at my head, throws its body back and forth, spitting at me and trying to bite whichever arm I use to pin her down.

She reaches for the door and goes to open it and I grab her

arm, pulling it away, and it clamps Evie's stale teeth around my wrist.

I retract my arm instinctively as I yelp, then quickly stop her from another attempt to open the door.

I move my body on top of her chest, using my body weight to pin her down, but it's strong, and it continues to fight and kick and thrash. I press harder, and think I have it under control—but just as the thought enters my mind, it swings an arm into my chest and sends me upwards, slamming me into the roof of the car.

My spine throbs and my arm aches, but I mustn't let it get out, I mustn't let it stop Grace driving—I *must* keep it under control.

There are sirens in the distance, growing louder.

It smirks and sings playfully, "*They are coming to get you-hoo...*"

It thrashes again, and I grab Evie's arms, and it out-muscles me and I let go and grab her again, and we do this over and over, Deumus forcing me to momentarily lose my grip; each little incident leaving me desperately trying to regain control.

The demon's murmurs accompany Grace's sniffs. She's not handling this well. I don't blame her. But she's doing what I need her to—she's driving without attracting attention.

The sirens are getting louder.

It grins at me, then throws itself at the window, battering against it whilst screaming, "*Help! Help!*"

I put my arm around its throat and pull it down. I lay on top of it, my arms wrapped tightly around Evie's chest, trying to contain her thrashing limbs.

The flashing lights illuminate the car in blue as they pass us.

Its fist strikes my side, and I lose my grip, and it forces its way out of my arms and rolls over me. It climbs on top of me, pinning me down. I struggle, and it places a hand on my head, and I am no longer in the car.

I am in a bedroom.

April is on the bed, naked and sweaty, a man over her—possibly Oscar?—heaving as he pushes himself deeper inside of her. She moans in pleasure as the man gets quicker, and the moans grow louder and he grunts and I hate seeing this—the body I've craved seeing, in ecstasy from another man—it is torment—I try to look away—but I can't look away—it won't let me—and April and the man climax together in a moment of perfect euphoria.

I swipe her arms off my forehead, and I am back in the car, and she is grinning.

More sirens approach. Police cars become visible through the window. Deumus tries to wave Evie's arms at the window, but I grab her around the waist and drag her down and her hands touch my skin and I'm five-years-old again.

In the living room.

Dad's television is surrounded by VHS tapes. The remains of a cigarette rests in an ashtray, smoke rising into the air. Thuds through the hallway warn me about what is about to happen.

Oh, God, where do I go? Where do I hide? How do I get away?

It's too late.

He's stood in the doorway, drool around his mouth, that dead-eyed expression he always has when he's wasted.

"Please..." My voice hasn't broken yet, and it sounds tiny and insignificant. "Please don't..."

He snarls and laughs.

"You are pathetic," he tells me, his voice grumbling, and he stumbles forward.

I try to dodge him and make it out of the door, but he grabs me by the hair and throws me back.

"You killed my wife..."

I cry and I beg him not to do this, but he tells me that I'm worthless, and my life means nothing, and I'll amount to shit, and he strikes me, hard, in my belly, and this is the side of him I hated.

I loved him, but I hated this.

In the morning, he'll apologise.

The bruises will be hidden.

He'll take me to a fast-food restaurant of my choice to make up for it, and he'll smile, and we will be happy again.

But for now, I am simply wincing at his every movement, afraid of another assault.

"Stop!"

I bat her arm away.

More police sirens pass.

The car is travelling at some speed. Or does it just feel that way?

It looks down at me, grinning.

"*I never knew there were so many wonders left in your mind...*"

I go to react, then remind myself not to—it wants a reaction. It grows stronger with every bit of pain it causes.

The car slows down and comes to a halt. We are at a set of traffic lights.

I lean up and notice that there is a police car behind us.

Just as it goes to wave her arms, I grab it around the waist and keep it below the window and its hand touches my neck and I'm a teenager, watching my foster parents sit in their dressing gowns as they stare gormlessly at a bunch of idiots shouting at each other on daytime television.

Eric is beside me. He's another foster kid. He's ten. He's not as tough as me. He can't stand up for himself. That's why they put their cigarettes out on him instead.

And I just watch.

I sit in the armchair and watch.

I could stop them. I could throw a punch, tell them to back off, protect the child. I could end the boy's misery right now. It's trauma he'll remember for the rest of his life, but it's still early enough to save him.

But I don't.

I shut up.

And I just sit there.

And I watch.

Why do I just watch?

I bat its arm away and keep it pinned on the car seat.

The police car behind us puts on its sirens.

"Shit!"

I prepare my answers and my excuses and my pleas—then it overtakes us and accelerates into the distance.

And I breathe a sigh of relief.

It tries to reach its hands up again, to make contact with my head, and I pin them down, and it wriggles and fights, but I manage to keep it down.

I look out the window. We are next to the wood. A large clump of trees huddled together, so vast one could easily get lost in them. There is no telling how vast the wood is.

But this means we're close.

The church must be around the corner.

Deumus appears subdued. Taking a break. Resting for a moment as it leers up at me. I take the opportunity to gather my strength, to breathe, to calm my mind.

And I realise how stupid I am to think it's taking a rest as it punches my chest and knocks me off.

By the time I've regathered myself, it has opened the car door.

I grab Evie's foot, but it slithers out of my grasp, and she sprints across the road and into the woods.

Dammit.

"Get my bag and follow us!" I shout at Grace as I rush out of the car.

I follow it into the darkness of the woods. It isn't long until I'm lost amongst a mass of trees, searching desperately for the demon.

If it is free, it will kill.

And Evie will be forced to watch as her hands take another's life.

And so I move deeper into the woods, peering into the night, hoping for a flicker in the darkness—anything that will tell me where Evie is.

TWENTY-EIGHT

I stride in the direction she went, but it takes less than a minute for me to realise I've lost her.

Every rustle attracts my attention.

Every snap of a twig, every whisper on the wind, every chirp of a grasshopper makes me turn my head.

The moonlight casts a little light, but I rely on my senses to point me in the right direction. I listen for footsteps on leaves. I try to pick up the faint aroma of body odour or rotten eggs. I touch the trees and feel for moisture from a sweaty palm.

I stay still. If I keep going, I could end up walking in the wrong direction, and I'd end up much further away from her.

I look over my shoulder. The road is so far away that I can no longer hear cars. The outline of the trees rises up into the sky, and their thick leaves are a silhouette in front of the moon. I am stranded in the middle of the woods, lost in the shadows, and I don't know where I am.

I take a step forward and a cobweb covers my face. I pull it off and spit it out.

I reach my arms out for trees and use them as a guide. My

ankle bumps into a log, and I step over it. I hear a bird some-where, a chirp that would sound lovely in the light, but sounds ominous in the dark.

I consider calling out for Evie. For Deumus. But that would just give my position away.

Although I have no doubt it knows where I am.

It could have run off. Hidden. Sprinted as far from me as it could.

But I doubt it.

Truth is that demons might be evil, wicked, and malevo-lent—but they are rarely cowards.

The demon will want to face me.

It has already defeated me several times. It has the power over me that I wish to have over it. It will not want to let me go, and I can feel its beady eyes staring at me; though I can't be certain.

I just feel it.

It's hunting me.

It's watching. Waiting.

It wants to kill me.

And it could, too. It's strong. Strong enough to pin me down and suffocate me, or slice its nail along my throat, or maybe even press its thumbs against my temple and make me end things myself.

I am merely a lost wanderer in the darkness. I am the prey, and it is the predator.

Why did I chase it in here?

But what was I supposed to do? Let it kill someone else?

Besides, what would I really be losing if I died? What loss would it be to the world?

There'll be an extra crate of beer on the supermarket shelf. An extra council flat for a family to live in. Another tragic story for someone else to tell.

Maybe death would be the perfect answer.

But I find myself defying my logic. I find myself, as perplexing as it is, wanting to live.

I need to beat this demon and take revenge for the memories it's forced me to relive.

If only I could see a damn thing.

A twig snaps. I turn to my right. Stare into the blackness.

A hushed giggle passes by, so quiet that I could be mistaken.

I turn around, peering toward a sound that could easily be a brush of wind.

"Evie?"

I step forward, keeping my hands on the trees, moving slowly, feeling for what is in front of me with my foot before I place it down.

"I know you're there."

It's not much of a threat.

As I walk further toward the sound, I step further into fog; white mist hides my surroundings. I reach my arm out and I can barely see my hand.

"*I see you...*"

I turn to my left.

Or did it come from my right?

"*You're going to die...*"

I turn around.

It was behind me.

Definitely behind me.

"*You are such a fool...*"

I turn around again, sure that I have the right direction, and walk further the fog, just as it wants me to, stretching my arms into the unknown.

I'm shaking.

I feel afraid in a way I haven't felt for a long time.

It's the same fear I felt hiding behind the sofa when Dad arrived home; I'd listen to him knocking shoes off the shoe rack and shouting at them before he started demanding to know where I am.

I hate that fear.

That fear makes me feel like a child.

It makes me feel like I'm back there again—but maybe I never actually left.

"*You aren't going to win...*"

It's straight ahead. I know it. It sounded more definite that time; I am sure.

I pick up my pace, trying not to bump into anything, lifting my legs high to avoid logs, pulling myself forward with the trees, adrenaline forcing me onward.

"*Big, bad exorcist likes to play with demons...*"

I pick up my stride, walking quicker, surging, sure of where it is.

"*I'm going to kill April next, you know.*"

It wasn't a whisper. It sounded like the voice of a posh old man; one that makes me freeze.

Then its face is in front of me, and I am on the floor, and I am shaking, my arms and legs thrashing around, completely out of my control.

I can just about make out its eyes.

I try to say something, but only foam comes out of my mouth.

Its silhouette hovers above me, the faint outline of its limbs pointing in obscure directions, shifting with each breath.

It grins, knowing it is about to finish me, and it presses its thumbs against my head, and I'm back in that damn garage again, watching Dad prepare his noose, over and over.

This is my Hell, and it is where she plans to leave me.

TWENTY-NINE

The rain pounds against the garage door, accompanied by crashes of thunder and flashes of lightning shining through the crack beneath it.

Dad stands over a box of Mum's stuff. He looks at the photo frame.

This time, I do approach him.

This time, I've had enough.

"Dad, stop it!"

I sound like a child. I look down at my hands. The wrinkles and scars are missing. My palms are soft, and my fingers are small. I'm young again.

Dad shakes his head. Looks at the photo.

This time, I look over his shoulder at the photo. It's of Dad and Mum, and they both look young, maybe early twenties. Hope in their eyes. Arms around each other. They look happy in the way I've imagined April and myself being happy.

"Dad, please don't make me live through this again..."

He puts the photo frame back in the box. Closes it. This time, I see his face up close—and it is not sadness or solace I see in it. It is shame and weariness. He is tired, and he hates himself.

I even hear him mutter, in a way that would have been inaudible to me before, "I'm sorry, Moses..."

"It's fine, Dad! It's okay! I forgive you!"

I don't know if I'm invisible to him, or if he's just ignoring me, but he turns without so much as glancing in my direction and looks at the noose.

The damn noose.

A simple looped rope. Something so insignificant that will come to mean so much.

He closes his eyes for a moment, then opens them, and walks toward the chair with small steps.

"Dad! For fuck's sake, don't do this!"

I put an arm out, and I can touch him. I push him back, and I do it with all of my body weight. He doesn't react to me —he just keeps walking against me, and he does so easily. I'm a kid again. I don't have the strength to stop him.

"Please..."

I give in to the tears. I've fought them too much. Dad taught me that a man doesn't cry, yet I see it in his eyes. The sobs. The sniffs. Maybe it's just another thing he lied about.

He steps onto the chair. I try to pull him down, but I'm just a gentle nudge against his leg. He takes the noose and places it around his neck.

And he has his hesitation.

"No..." he says. "I can't do this to you..."

And Deumus appears behind him in Evie's body, with her greasy hair and her contorted limbs, and just as Dad is about to take the noose off, she pushes the chair away.

"No!"

I try to lift Dad's legs up to stop him from suffocating, but my child's arms can do nothing to help.

And Deumus stands there, cackling as Dad suffocates.

And I am forced to watch. Witnessing the last moments of his life, the look on his face as he regrets everything, as he realises it's the end, as death comes closer, until eventually, he's gone.

I bow my head.

There is a movement by the boxes.

I lift my head again, and Dad is no longer hanging from the noose. He opens the box and stares at the picture of Mum again.

"Oh, God, no..."

He puts the photo frame back in the box and turns to the noose.

Is this my eternal torment?

Am I to relive this over and over?

But I am not dead. I know I am still alive. This is just what she's doing to my mind.

And I realise what's happening.

Why she's doing this.

The only way to stop it... is to die.

The only way for me to stop reliving this moment is to end my life and end its repetition.

But I refuse to die.

Though I can't see the alternative.

Do I just stay here? Seeing this over and over whilst my mortal mind goes crazy? Once my mind is gone, my body will be locked up and left to whither away in a home or a psychiatric hospital or wherever they put people who are too insane to be accepted by the world.

Dad walks toward the chair.

And I fall to my knees and cry.

I need the strength to endure this. To make it stop.

But I don't think I'm that strong.

He stands on the chair.

"No... I can't do this to you..."

He goes to step down and I cannot do anything but watch as Deumus pushes the chair away and I have to see his face again, the same twitches, the same flickers of anger, the same contortion of despair, the one I have already witnessed over and over, until he chokes and dies.

I cover my head in my hands. Try not to give Deumus the weeps it desires, though I'm unable to do anything but.

And this time I just listen.

Listen to the box being opened. The steps toward the noose. "No... I can't do this to you..." The swipe of the chair and the asphyxiation and the suffering until it is done, and it starts all over again.

And I look up.

And he stares at the picture of him and Mum.

And this time I am angry.

My fists clench. My body tenses. My heart races.

My lips curl into a sneer.

I am fed up. This demon wants a war, and I am laying down and surrendering and I need to stop it and I need to quit being so miserable—and I need to get pissed off.

He walks to the noose. He stands on the chair. He puts it around his neck. And he changes his mind.

"No... I can't do this to you..."

And Deumus appears behind him.

Her demented visage, her haggish appearance, her unwavering confidence.

Only this time, I am the one who screams, letting out a roar as I charge forward.

She goes to kick out the chair—only this time; she doesn't.

Because I grab her around the waist and take her to the floor.

She fights and she squirms, but I hold her down, and I refuse to let her be stronger than me in my own memory.

I am in charge here.

Not *you.*

I look over my shoulder as I pin her down.

Dad takes the noose from around his neck. He steps from the chair, and he kicks it across the room in a bout of anger, then he falls to his knees and buries his head in his hands.

I look down, and Deumus is gone.

I rush over to Dad, and I kneel beside him.

"It's okay," I say, placing my arms around him.

He looks up, confused, his eyes red.

"What are you doing here?" he asks. "I thought you were at your friends?"

"I came home early."

"Why?"

"To... to see you."

He cries again. He puts his arms around me and grabs my t-shirt and holds me tight, and I put my arms around him, my thin, gangly body embracing him back, and I let him cry into my collar.

"It's okay, Dad," I say.

"No..." he whimpers. "No... It's not..."

He lifts his head up. Puts his hands on my cheeks. Looks at me in a way he rarely did.

"I have been a really poor dad."

"It's okay, you–"

"No, it's not okay. It's not. I shouldn't have blamed you for your mother's death. I shouldn't have held it against you. I shouldn't have kept drinking."

"I know."

"I hurt you, and I shouldn't have, and I am sorry. I am really sorry."

I don't want to leave.

I know it's all in my mind, and I have a battle to fight in reality, but this is a moment I have longed to have, and I don't care if it's real or not, I just can't leave it.

"You are a much better man than I, Moses. You really are."

I wipe my eyes. "Why didn't you get help? Why did you kill yourself instead of... I don't know..."

"I just couldn't bear being the kind of man who would hurt his son."

"But you could have changed. You could have become someone I respected, you could have..."

He shushes me. Strokes my hair back. Smiles in that way I so rarely saw him smile.

"You need to go back now," he tells me.

"I don't want to."

"You must. Evie needs you."

"But I can't win..."

He shakes his head. "You just have."

"What?"

"You've shown the creature that you're stronger than it thought you are. Now, you need to finish it."

"But what about you?"

He shakes his head. "Don't worry about me."

"But–"

"I'll always be here."

He stands. Sighs. Steps back.

"Why couldn't you have said this to me when it was real?"

He shrugs. "Because life isn't like that."

I go to answer back, but he's already fading away, and my eyes are opening, and I am in the woods.

I push myself to my feet. A flashlight appears behind me. It's Grace with my bag, and her light illuminates Evie's body.

Deumus doesn't look as confident now.

"You don't have control over me anymore," I tell it. "And I think it's time that you leave."

THIRTY

Grace hands me my crucifix and directs the light on Evie's body. I grip it, its edges digging into my palm, holding it toward the demon and enjoying its first look of dread since the battle began.

The grin has gone, replaced by a grimace. It backs away from me, sneering as it realises how humiliating it is to lose.

"That you spare us, that you pardon us, that you bring us to true penance!"

It turns, and it tries to run away, but on my command, "You will stay here, Deumus!" it falls over a branch and lands on her knees.

"That you govern and preserve your holy church, that you preserve our Holy Father, and all ranks in the holy religion!"

I stride forward, until I am stood over it, my feet either side of its waist, and I lower my cross, slowly, watching it cower as the symbol it fears grows closer.

"That you humble the enemies of the Holy Church, that you give peace and true concord to our rulers!"

I lower my arm until the cross meets Evie's skin, providing a satisfying *tsst*. I don't like that this could hurt Evie, but I love that it could hurt the demon—and, if Evie wishes to be free, she needs to endure a little pain.

This won't work unless Evie fights too.

"That you restore to the unity of the church all that has strayed from the truth, and that you confirm and preserve us in your holy service!"

I've never cared much for these words.

They imply that this particular denomination of this particular religion is the only one, and we must save all other religions from their error. The truth is that all religions have their own services and processes for exorcising demons—and all of them have worked. It isn't the prayers that matter—it's the meaning behind them. It's the strength I feel as I bellow the words and the power they have upon my enemy.

It is how it makes The Shit of Hell tremble at my feet like a useless coward.

"That you deliver our souls and the souls of our brethren, just as you saved us from everlasting damnation, save this servant of God from this bastard demon!"

The gentle breeze grows heavier, and the gusts grow stronger, until the wind is battering against me. The flashlight shakes as Grace tries to resist being thrown about by the wind, but the force of it is such that it is difficult to stand still.

I am not deterred—this means I'm winning.

"Just as you gave us fruits of the earth, eternal rest to the faithful departed, and that you guide our world toward peace—guide this demon from your servant and let her be free!"

My hair whips back and forth. My jacket bustles. Leaves spin around my feet. The trees rattle, branches quiver, and faint shadows cast by the moonlight move quickly over us.

"Haughty men have risen against me, and fierce men seek my life—but I turn back the evil on my foes, and I command you, beast, leave this body!"

Its face changes. It fights its vulnerabilities. It resists my commands. It turns onto its front and pushes itself to its feet.

No. I can't let it gather strength. I can't let it recuperate.

"In your faithfulness I destroy them, freely I offer you sacrifice, and I will praise your name as you rescue this child from its tormenter!"

Evie's arms shake. Her loose clothes, sticky with perspiration, batter around her body. But, despite the wind and the strength of my command, it pushes itself to its feet and takes a few moments to gather itself.

Somehow, it's resisting.

Is the demon so far embedded in this girl's body that I truly cannot save her?

I tell myself to keep trying. Keep giving the prayers. It is fighting its weaknesses; I must do the same.

"For you, whose nature is merciful and forgiving, accept our nature and accept our prayer that this servant of yours may be granted safe passage back to its body!"

I can hear it in my voice.

Doubt.

A minute ago, it was strong. Now it sounds like it's pretending to be strong.

I try not to be deterred, but it's standing in front of me, and it's grinning again, and its fists are clenching, and its body is tensing, and it looks like it's getting ready for another fight.

I thought I was winning, but I barely bruised it.

"I command you, unclean spirit, along with your minions attacking this servant of God, leave us!"

But there's not as much conviction in my voice. Before, I had strength you can't fake, and now I'm forcing it, and it is doing nothing.

I take a deep breath, strengthen my grip on my crucifix, direct it at Deumus, and I try again.

"By the mysteries of the incarnation, the passion, resurrection, and His ascension, I command you, leave this girl!"

It steps toward me. The beam of light from the torch shakes. I feel Evie's fear, and it fuels it, so I try not to give it any of my own.

It pauses, inches from my face, and snarls, cocky, saliva dripping down her chin.

"By the descent of the Holy Spirit and the coming of the Lord, I command you–"

It throws its fist hard into my chest, and it sends me from my feet, soaring across the woods, until I land metres away, on my side, clutching my belly as I try to breathe.

I rub my chest, fighting the pain, and roll onto my back.

It steps toward Grace.

"Run, Grace!"

I've seen what these things do to the parents.

I saw it in the last exorcism I was part of.

And I really don't want to see it again.

"Run!"

But she's not running. She can't. The demon stares into her eyes, and Grace cannot move.

I push myself to my knees, determined to help her, but I'm too dizzy. I try to stand, and I fall again.

The demon places Evie's palm around Grace's neck and lifts her off the ground.

"Come on!" I urge myself.

I rub my head, then use a nearby tree to guide me to my feet.

The demon's grip tightens around Grace's throat, smiling as Evie's mother suffocates, enjoying her splutter and hopeless fight. Grace tries to pull Evie's fingers away, tries to batter at her daughter's arm, but it's too strong.

I run forward, and I fall, landing in wet leaves, and I push myself to my feet again.

Grace's resistance grows weaker. She struggles, but not as much. Any minute now, she'll lose consciousness.

And death will follow shortly after.

I take a few deep breaths until I stop wheezing. I try to keep my balance, stumbling from one foot to the other, until I can finally stand tall, and I approach the demon.

Grace's eyes close, and I scream, "No!" as I charge toward it, and knock into Evie's chest, forcing Deumus to drop Grace.

Deumus narrows its eyes into a glare, and I shove my hand against Evie's heart, hold it there, and demand to speak to Evie.

Demand to speak to the true owner of this body.

Demand to see the one who's had to suffer through this.

A blinding white light follows.

I turn my head away, cover my eyes, shielding them.

When I open my eyes again, I can't quite believe what I see.

THIRTY-ONE

"Evie?"

We are in a dungeon. The air is moist, there is a distant drip, and the room is cold. The walls are made of stone, and the floor is bumpy and uncomfortable.

I know we aren't actually in a dungeon. We are simply in the environment through which Evie perceives her entrapment; a cold, damp room, with nowhere comfortable to rest, and very little natural light.

Evie sits in the corner, huddled in a ball, shaking. She wears a grubby, torn nightie. Her hair is matted. Her bare feet are filthy. But there are no fresh scars or marks from the demon, just faded wounds and blemishes that have become part of her skin—this is Evie's soul; or, at least, it is the state that her soul is in.

I kneel before her and place my hands on her cheeks. She flinches away.

"It's okay," I assure her. "I'm not going to hurt you."

She looks up at me, timidly. Tears in her eyes. Weakness on her face. She can barely lift her head.

"My name is Moses," I tell her.

"I know..." she whimpers. "I've seen you..."

"You have?"

"You were trying to fight... *her*."

"I've been trying to save you, Evie."

Evie goes to reply, then her eyes fill up with tears and she turns away.

"It's okay," I tell her. "It's okay now. I'm here to help."

"You don't understand..."

"Don't understand what?"

"She..." Evie looks up at me, months of painful solitude evident across her frail body. "She told me she loved me... That she wanted to be with me..."

I smile sympathetically. "That's what they do, Evie. They make you think they love you. They make you think they are helping. Then they take away everything you hold dear."

"Mummy... is Mummy okay?"

I pause. I'm not sure. "I think so."

"I didn't hurt her, did I?"

"You didn't do a thing. Deumus is the name of the thing that's taken your body—and I think your mother's okay."

By okay, I mean *alive*. I ignore the trauma and the mental servitude she has suffered, and will continue to suffer, should this ever be over. But she is still breathing, I think, and that will give Evie the strength she needs.

I hope.

"We need to go now, Evie."

She vigorously shakes her head and turns away.

"Come on," I urge her.

"No..."

"Why not?"

"She will get me."

"She won't."

"I—I'm scared..."

I sigh. Look around. I don't know how much time we have, but I can't rush this.

"I'm scared too, Evie."

She looks up at me, surprised. "Really?"

"Oh yeah. All the time."

"Of Deumus?"

"Of... everything."

"I thought you're too old to be scared."

I smile. "I'm too old for a lot of things, but you never stop being scared. You just pretend better."

"What are you scared of?"

What a question. One I'm not sure we have time for. But she won't move unless she trusts me.

"My dad," I say.

"Your dad hurts you?"

"He did. He killed himself. And I am so, so scared of turning out like him."

She nods. It seems to help.

"I'm scared of not being enough. That the woman I love will never see me as a hero—just an annoyance. A burden. That I will never amount to the great man she still holds onto."

I sigh. Fight back tears. I didn't realise how much of this was inside of me.

"And I am worried that I will disappoint everyone. All the time. That I will never be enough."

"And how do you stop being afraid?"

I take her hand. I stroke it with my other, and her body seems to open up to me. "I don't."

"You don't?"

"You don't stop being afraid, Evie. You become afraid, and then—then you do it anyway. All we can do is fight. And you need to keep fighting."

She shakes her head.

"I can't."

"Yes, you can."

She shakes her head again. "No, I tried, and it just got harder, it became nastier, and it said it would hurt my mum and—"

"That was before I was here. Now we can do it together."

I stand. Hold out my hand. She doesn't take it, so I don't wait. I grab hold of her wrist and pull her to her feet.

Then, just as we turn to go, she yelps, and her eyes grow wide as she sees something over my shoulder.

I turn, and there it is.

Four horns. Four hooked teeth. Rooster legs leading to hooked feet. Its claws flexing and opening, eager for a soul to crush.

Deumus.

Thirty-Two

"We are leaving this dungeon," I tell it. "And you are leaving her body."

It flinches.

It doesn't grin, leer, sneer, snort, laugh, or make any other arrogant gesture designed to intimidate. It just flinches.

Which is how I know it's almost over.

I take Evie's hand and I try to pull her up. She is resistant, staring adamantly at the demon, her face gripped with terror. I pull harder and force her to her feet, and she falls against the wall like she's not used to standing up.

"*You can't have her,*" it says.

I laugh at it, as mockingly as I can.

"You're done," I tell it. "It's time for you to go home."

Its face curls, and it lets out a moan that turns into a roar.

But it's still pitiful, like a toddler trying to scare a grown man.

It does nothing.

I hold Evie up, trying to keep her steady. She balances precariously, and with just a little support, she stays upright.

She does not stop staring at the beast.

"Look at me," I tell her.

She doesn't.

"I said look this way—at me."

I grab her face and turn it toward me.

"There's nothing to be afraid of anymore," I tell her. "It's lost."

It steps toward us. "No, I haven't."

I'm about to retort, when I realise it's right.

I've stopped it from exploiting my fears.

I've stopped it from killing Grace.

And I've weakened its grip over this girl's body.

But there is still one more fight that needs to be won, and it's not my fight.

It's Evie's.

I put my fingers beneath her chin and keep her eyes on mine. I smile at her, warmly, like a caring older brother, and there is a break in her terror where confusion sets in. How could I be smiling at a time like this?

"It's up to you now, kid," I tell her.

She looks perplexed. Then her expression changes to hope as she realises she could end this, then to terror as she realises it's up to her.

"*Sit down, Evie.*"

Her lip trembles, and she goes to sit back down. I grab her shoulders and hold her upright.

"*Evie, I said sit down.*"

"Tell it no."

She turns to it. Her eyes narrow. She gets ready to be strong, only to find that she can't, and she looks back at me again.

"This is the only way you'll be free."

"*Am I stuttering? Evie, I demand you sit down!*"

She hovers, somewhere between lowering and standing, and I can see her arms shaking, and I try to hold them still.

"Do it, Evie."

She shakes her head—not in defiance, but in despair; she cannot do it.

Then I add, "Your mother is waiting," and her eyes light up. Amid her pain and fear, there is something more powerful that flickers in her eyes.

"Is she?" Evie asks.

"She's really missing you," I tell her. "She can't wait to see you."

"*He is trying to poison you. I am the one who saved you, not him. Now—sit—down!*"

She looks over my shoulder and, with a voice so quiet I can barely hear it, tries to push out a feeble, "No."

Deumus chuckles, and Evie almost backs down until I tell her, "Again, Evie."

Evie stares at the demon. Glaring. Her hands grip my arms, and she forces herself to stand upright.

"No," she says, a little stronger.

"Again."

"No!" she says, shouting.

"*Evie, I told you to–*"

"No! No, no, no, no!"

Deumus looks bemused.

And, upon finding that there are no repercussions to saying no, Evie stops using me to hold herself up, and she takes a large step forward.

"*Don't be so pathetic, Evie.*"

"Me? Pathetic? You are the one who's pathetic!"

She strides toward it, and it backs away, and this is how we win—the weak will always cower from the strong.

"You need me to survive in this world. You are a parasite. You can't even hurt me unless you make me hurt myself. Now leave. Leave!"

It shakes with fury, rage growing, clouds snorting through its nostrils, its horns looming larger.

But Evie is a brilliant young woman, defiant in the face of its tormentor, and she does not back down.

"Go! Leave me! Stop leaching off good people!"

"*But... I love you...*"

And there it is—it's final, weak attempt. If aggression doesn't work, and it can no longer induce pain, and it can't dominate her—then it will try to convince its victim that it loves them, just as it said it did at the beginning.

And Evie sees right through it.

"Well, I do not love you."

Its eyes narrow, it reaches out a claw, and it grabs Evie around the neck. It lifts her from the ground, and she struggles to breathe.

"*Fine. If I can't have your body, I can at least have your soul!*"

It squeezes her throat harder and harder.

I step forward.

I take hold of Evie's hand.

"It can't kill you if you don't let it," I tell her, slowly and calmly. "You're almost there."

And, just like that, she stops suffocating. It squeezes her throat, harder and harder, but she just breathes, finding the demon's claw to have no effect.

The demon, shocked and horrified by its lack of power, drops her and stands back.

"No," she tells it.

She stands tall.

"No!"

She runs toward it and barges into its chest, screaming, "*No!*"

And my eyes open.

THIRTY-THREE

The moon is the first thing I see.

It's directly above me, and it takes me a moment to realise that I'm still in the woods, lying on my back, staring at the faint light amongst the darkness.

Am I awake?

Am I even alive?

I wiggle my toes. They seem to work. I flex my fingers. Stretch my hands. Move my arms.

I have a pounding headache, but I can deal with that. I push myself up and look around. The flashlight is on the floor, and there is a silhouette behind it, hunched over, jolting with each sob it gives.

"Grace?" I say.

She lifts her head, surprised. "Mo?"

"Grace, what's going on?"

"I—I thought you were gone."

"I'm fine. Where's Evie?"

Grace picks up the torch and points it at Evie, lying face down a few metres away.

"Shine the torch on her," I instruct. I crawl toward her,

dragging myself through the mud. I get a head rush, but I don't pause. I can't waste any time.

I arrive at Evie's side, the back of her head lit by the artificial glow, and I move her onto her back.

Her face is still pale, but it's different. It's more human. I feel confident that it's worked, that we rid her of the demon.

But her eyes aren't opening.

Were we too late?

I put my ear by her lips and wait for breath to brush against it.

Maybe Deumus managed to take her soul. Maybe all that's left is an empty vessel. If so, there's no chance of reviving her —but we still need to try.

"Grace, she needs CPR."

Grace barely moves.

"Grace, you're a nurse, you can do this better than me —come on!"

She hesitates.

"We're running out of time."

Finally, she comes round, and she rushes to Evie's side. I take the light from her and shine it on Evie.

Grace interlocks her fingers, and places the heels of her hands against the breastbone over Evie's heart. Using her body weight, she presses down on her daughter's chest.

"Keep going, Grace!" I tell her, and Grace nods.

She has to focus.

She has to bring her back.

Please, let her bring Evie back.

She keeps pressing down on Evie's chest, over and over, trying to force her heart into beating.

After another half a minute of this, Grace tilts Evie's head back, lifts her chin with two fingers, and pinches her nose. She takes a deep breath, covers Evie's mouth with hers, and blows. I see Evie's chest rising, and it gives me hope.

After two breaths, Grace returns to pumping on her chest.

I go to phone 999, but it's pointless. I don't know how to tell them where to look. We are in the middle of woods in the dead of night, and my time is better spent supporting Grace, rather than hopelessly directing paramedics who will inevitably arrive too late.

Grace pauses for a moment and looks at Evie's body.

For what, I don't know.

A reaction?

A sign that Deumus hasn't won?

A flicker of the eyelids?

Evie gives us nothing.

Grace continues, determined, refusing to admit that Evie might be dead. Interlocking her fingers. Pressing down with the heel of her hands. Doing this over and over for about half a minute, then pinching Evie's nose. Lifting her chin. Breathing into her mouth.

Grace does this again.

Then again.

Still, nothing.

Still, Evie does not move.

Only when I am wondering whether it's time to give up, trying to decide how to tell Grace that it's a lost cause, I see it.

The flicker of the eyelids.

Evie's still in there.

She's still fighting Deumus.

We must keep going.

And so, with renewed vigour, Grace persists.

Pumping with the heels of her hands.

Lifting Evie's chin. Breathing into Evie's mouth.

Over and over, hoping for a reaction.

Until we finally get one, and Evie coughs into her mother's mouth, and Grace sits back, and I fall to my knees; a rush of relief and happiness and repressed fear and a million other emotions I can't quite comprehend force me to my knees, then to my back.

Grace grabs her daughter and brings her close and wraps her arms around her and cries, and tells her she loves her, and says how grateful she is, and I just lie there, the world spinning, grateful to have won.

I know I'm going to need to regather my strength. I'll need to carry her until we find a way out of the woods, then locate the nearest hospital. But for these few minutes, I rest.

And my body releases itself from all the tension.

We did it.

We actually did it.

And soon I can go to bed, and maybe even sleep through the night.

I know, crazy idea, right?

But hey, if I'm able to beat Deumus, maybe I can also find a way to fall asleep.

Epilogue

The sound of the duct tape echoes around the empty flat, and I cut the strip of tape off once it has sealed the box shut.

It didn't take long to pack up my belongings, nor did I have to find many boxes to do it. Most of these boxes, containing stained crockery, half empty jars of coffee, and clothes that I've had for too long, will be left outside the charity shop five minutes down the road. I have all I need inside my rucksack. Pants, socks, t-shirts, a spare pair of jeans, a few toiletries, and my only picture of Dad. I threw most pictures away when I was a teenager, but one fell beneath the bedsheets of my seventh foster home—and I was grateful when I found it a few months later. It's of me and Dad, in the 1965 Ford Mustang, taken by an instant camera Dad was given as a gift—he used that camera all the time, until he vomited on it in a drunken stupor and it stopped working. I look young, and my hair is scruffy, and my clothes are too big, but Dad looks just as I remember him. We are both smiling at the camera, and although I can't retrieve the memory, it looks like a good one.

I decide that I'm glad it's the only picture I have left—as it is exactly how I want to remember us.

I still haven't decided what to do with the remaining bottles of whiskey, or the last few beers in the fridge. Whether I will drink them, throw them away, or pack them in the inside compartment of my motorbike for later, I don't quite know yet.

The motorbike is a recent addition. After I took on the demon, April insisted the Church paid me for the service I provided. They weren't happy about it, and I insisted I did not want a penny from them, but they reluctantly put a generous amount of money in my account—enough for me to purchase my new vehicle, and to not have to rely on a 'real' job for a few months.

I said it wasn't necessary, but that's just April. She thinks of nothing but kindness.

I lean against the sink and fold my arms, wondering whether I should indulge in a modicum of nostalgia. I didn't live here for long, and I didn't make many happy memories between the thin, crumbling walls. In fact, most of the memories I have here are bad. Losing the car, getting the shit beaten out of me, and repeatedly failing to help Evie.

But I learned a few lessons here, I guess, whatever they were, and I should be grateful for the experience.

The toilet flushes and, a moment later, April walks out. I glimpse my reflection in the bathroom mirror as she opens the door, and I notice how I have aged a lot, and April has not aged at all.

She leans against the wall and folds her arms, echoing my stance. She looks at me, and we share a comfortable silence. I so rarely find a person who I can share a comfortable silence with, and it makes me a little sad when she ends it.

"Where are you going to go?" she asks.

I shrug. "Don't know."

"Why don't you come back with me?"

I drop my head.

"I know, I know," she says before I can reply. "You don't agree with the Church and all that. But, honestly, whoever agrees with their bosses? At least they clear up our mess so we don't have to."

"That's all they are, is it? Glorified cleaners?"

"Exactly."

"And what happens when you disagree with them? What do they do then?"

April doesn't answer. Instead, she huffs. Looks around and avoids looking at me. Suddenly, the silence isn't so comfortable anymore.

"Look, I—I'll continue to help people," I assure her.

"Then I will make sure the Church continues to pay you."

"I don't want their money."

"And I don't want you to starve."

"You don't have to keep taking care of me, April."

"Oh, because you did so well taking care of yourself? Look at what your life had become, Mo. Is it really—"

"Stop. Enough."

She drops her arms and turns as if she is going to leave, but doesn't. She can't. April could never end a conversation like this.

"I don't belong with your Sensitives, April."

"And what about me? Do you belong with me?"

I step forward, but do not enter her space.

"April, there's nothing I want more. But it's just not going to... That's why I have to..."

I try to explain, try to search for the words, but they don't arrive, and before either of us can continue the conversation, there is a gentle knock on the front door. I shuffle past April and open it. Grace stands there. She isn't wearing her dressing gown anymore. Instead, she is wearing nurse scrubs. She has a bit of makeup on. Not much, but enough that she looks a bit spritelier.

She beams at me and brings me in for a hug.

"I can't believe you're going," she says.

"I know. And what's with the outfit?"

She opens her arms to show off what she's wearing. "I started working again."

"At which hospital? Let me know, so I make sure I don't go there."

She laughs. I laugh. Then the laughter dies and there is silence. April appears over my shoulder.

"How's Evie?" she asks.

"Ask her yourself," Grace says, just as her front door opens.

The girl is almost unrecognisable.

Her skin has life and colour. She holds herself higher, rather than hunching over and shaking. I can smell the freshness in her clothes, and it makes me feel warm inside to see her so happy.

"Moses, I..." she says, then stops herself. "I just... I wanted to say–"

"Nothing," I interrupt. "You wanted to say nothing."

She smiles.

"We were wondering," Grace says, "if you would like to come over for tea?" She looks at April. "Both of you. A good-bye, thank you type of thing. Nothing too big, just some chicken and vegetables."

April begins to say, "We would love that," but before she can get the sentence out, I say, "I really can't. I have to get going."

Grace looks disappointed, but I'm not a good dinner guest. I don't hold conversation well, and honestly, right now, she thinks of me as a hero. As someone wonderful. I prefer that it's left that way.

We hug again, and we say our goodbyes, and they leave.

April and I carry the boxes to the charity shop without speaking, then I drop the keys off at the council office on the way back, and we stop at my motorbike. I take my helmet and get it ready to put on, but don't.

I feel like there are things I'm meant to say, but I'm not sure what they are.

I know she wants to beg me to stay, to berate me with reasons I should go back with her, of how I should use my gift to aid the Sensitives in their ongoing war with the devil.

But it's useless.

So she says the last thing she wants to say, but what she believes I want to hear.

Because that's April, and I wish I was capable of such kindness.

"I hope you find what you're looking for," she says.

"Thanks," I say.

She holds an arm out and we have one of those half-hearted, non-committal hugs, where we pat each other's back with one arm. It lasts for a moment, then I get on the motorbike.

"If you ever need our help," April says. "You know where we are."

I nod. Smile. Gaze at her. Take in those eyes and that skin and that hair and I hate myself for being such a bastard. I'm not sure why I'm being a bastard in this situation, but I'm pretty sure I am.

"See you later," I say.

She backs away and waves.

I put on the helmet, turn on the ignition, and drive away.

I don't know where I'm going, no idea what I'll do when I get there, or who I'm going to be when someone asks.

But I am pretty sure I'll figure it out.

For now, the possibilities are endless, and I have a gift I can use to help others.

Someday, maybe I'll even find somewhere I want to stay for more than a few months.

Maybe I'll even fall in love with someone else.

Or maybe I'll just find another demon that needs a good thrashing.

Hell, I'd settle on finding somewhere to have a good drink.

And so I enter the motorway with a rucksack on my back, wind against my body, and, inside my pocket, a crumpled photograph of two people whose lives were so full of opportunity.

And maybe that opportunity is still there. Maybe there's still a vast array of possibilities, fantastic things to be done, and a wonderful person to become.

I guess there's only one way to find out.

JOIN RICK WOOD'S READER'S GROUP...

And get three eBooks for free

Join at **www.rickwoodwriter.com/sign-up**

Book Two is Out in 2023

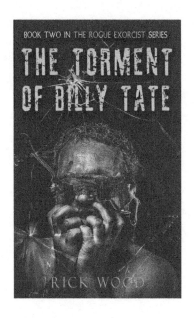

ALSO BY RICK WOOD

BLOOD SPLATTER BOOKS

18+

HAUNTED HOUSE

RICK WOOD

BOOK ONE IN THE SENSITIVES SERIES

THE SENSITIVES

RICK WOOD

Made in the USA
Monee, IL
20 April 2022

95071124R00163